Breathe

Look for these titles by
Donna Alward

Now Available:

The Girl Most Likely
Almost a Family
Sold To The Highest Bidder

Breathe

Donna Alward

To Jen

Don't forget to Breathe

Donna
xx

SAMHAIN
PUBLISHING

Samhain Publishing, Ltd.
577 Mulberry Street, Suite 1520
Macon, GA 31201
www.samhainpublishing.com

Editing by Heidi Moore
Cover by Kanaxa

First Samhain Publishing, Ltd. electronic publication: November 2010
First Samhain Publishing, Ltd. print publication: December 2011

Dedication

I have wonderful memories of camping and touring the Shuswap Lake area of British Columbia, and now that I live thousands of kilometers away I think of it with warmth and affection. Beautiful lake, fresh Okanagan fruit and home of Granite Creek Estate Winery—and its owner, Gary, who took the time to answer my questions and gave me their last bottle of Syrah.

In the words of my wonderful husband: The most beautiful place on earth.

Chapter One

Anna ground the stick down another gear, hit the gas and wondered why in the world Jace would choose to live in such a place. Tall stands of trees thwarted any hope of seeing past the ditches on the sides of the road. She took a quick, frantic glimpse down at the directions she'd printed out, narrowly missed making a right-angle turn, and sighed heavily. Normally she enjoyed getting away, doing new things. But today her patience was at near zero and dwindling rapidly.

"Mama?"

Damn. Matteo was awake. A quick turn of her head and she saw him rubbing his eyes, his nearly black hair flattened on one side where it had pressed against the seat. She turned her attention back to the road. "Quietly, Matteo," she whispered. "We're nearly there. Don't wake Aurelia, okay?"

"Mama, I'm *hungry*."

"I know, sweetie." Anna caught sight of a road sign that showed a bunch of grapes. Beneath it were the words "Two Willows Winery" and then "2 KM", and she let out a breath. Thank God, it wasn't much farther. It had been a long day.

It had been a long few months, when it came right down to it.

She pasted on a bright smile and made her voice light, despite the unease swirling around in her stomach. "Just a few more minutes and we'll be at Jace's, I promise." She'd be relieved to be at their destination...except that Jace had no idea they were coming. And she wasn't exactly sure how she was going to explain their sudden arrival, let alone ask for a place to stay. It was the height of presumption, thinking that Jace would welcome them with open arms.

The road snaked around another curve and inclined further. Anna kept both hands on the wheel to negotiate the turns. Uncle Jace indeed. Not that he'd been around more than a handful of times since Matteo had been born. He'd suddenly become so busy and important he didn't have time for the Morellis anymore. Not that she wasn't proud of his success...of course she was. But there had been times over the years she'd missed him terribly. She wondered why he'd kept away, and if it had anything to do with what had happened—and what hadn't—between them.

At the same time, a curl of dread spiraled through her stomach. She hadn't even given him any warning. Feeling trapped like a butterfly under glass, she'd needed to get away. Somewhere safe. In her head she knew that Jace's was the last place she should go. They had too much history. But her heart told her differently. Here she could hide for a little while. Ever since her husband's funeral she'd wanted to scream with the need to escape. And the only place she wanted to be was with Jace.

Which, of course, made absolutely no sense.

She braked and cranked the wheel around another sharp bend, cursing under her breath so that Matteo wouldn't hear. She wasn't familiar with the roads. The first hour of the drive had been quite pretty, route 97 as pleasant as she remembered. But climbing the narrow road to Jace's new winery was quite another matter. At home she knew the vineyard like the back of her hand. But she wasn't home any more. She was here and driving towards a new life. This was only the first step, a chance to regroup. A chance to get her feet beneath her once again.

Her old life was over. Stefano had seen to that, and playing the dutiful widow for appearances had taken its toll. Having to put on a false face of grief had exhausted her beyond anything she'd ever known. Because the truth of the matter was she'd been leaving him anyway, and knowing her remorse had little to do with his death caused more guilt and anguish than she could have anticipated.

Another small sign announced the entrance and she turned left, nervousness getting the best of her. She hadn't seen Jace in nearly a year, not since right after Aurelia had been born. She bit down on her lip as Matteo sighed from the backseat. Jace had brought Aurelia a stuffed lamb, fuzzy and white with a pink ribbon. And then he'd left again, without even visiting. She missed how they used to talk about old times, but for a very long time she'd felt he was putting a pleasant face on resentment. What she didn't understand was why. He'd been the one to walk away first, so where did all the resentment come from?

But it didn't matter. Right now, being a good mother to Matteo and Aurelia was her first priority. Coming to Jace's made sense on some level. She would be safe here for a while, hidden away until she could figure out what to do. Her father wasn't above strong-arming her to do what he wanted, but he would never follow her here. Jace's name wasn't even spoken in the Morelli household. Jace and Alex had remained friends, but Alex had branched out into the restaurant business on the lower mainland, out from under their father's thumb.

Anna envied him his independence.

Now she was ready to claim her own freedom. Surely Jace could put up with them for a few weeks. For all Jace's faults, he'd always said that if she needed anything, he'd be there. She'd never planned on taking him up on it. For a time she would have rather died than ask him for anything. But desperate times...

And it wasn't just for herself. The children would be away from the whispers and pitying looks of the household staff and their elitist circle of "friends". No one knew her here. They might have some sense of normalcy. Meanwhile, she could stay under the radar until she decided what it was she wanted to do.

"Mama, are we there yet?"

She couldn't help but smile softly at the plaintive question. She slowed the car and peered over her shoulder at Matteo, strapped into a car seat and blinking his round eyes at her.

"Yes, we're here. Just a moment, and I promise you can get out and run around."

She pulled out of the trees and into a small parking area that held one other vehicle. A shiny, silver Porsche 911 Carerra.

Jace's car.

Leave it to Jace to drive a two-seater bullet. She shouldn't be surprised. He'd always been one for toys. The flashier the better. It seemed nothing had changed. He had always been hungry for *things*. Briefly she wondered if all men thought of their value as the sum of their possessions. Certainly Stefano had. She remembered the sailboat he'd bought. In the end it had been his worst mistake. Anna knew better than most that things were just that. Material possessions. Certainly not enough to build a life on. She'd tried explaining that to Jace once, but he hadn't wanted to listen then either. The memory touched a hollow part within her.

The parking area was just below a large house, more like a lodge than a regular dwelling, built of reddish-stained logs.

As she pulled to a stop, Jace stepped out of a line of vines to her right. He halted and stared, his lips flattening with surprise at seeing her behind the wheel. No smile. No wave of greeting. And her stomach tumbled over itself.

She'd known him for so long she'd nearly forgotten how imposing he could be. His tall frame was lean and muscled, not overly large but exuding a confidence and power she'd always admired. But at this moment, the charming smile and manner she'd come to expect were absent. He almost looked angry now, mingled with surprise at her turning up so unexpectedly. She wrinkled her brow and glanced in the backseat. Matteo was already attempting to undo his seatbelt.

And with a stroke of perfect timing, Aurelia woke at the sudden lack of motion and started wailing at the top of her tiny lungs.

Anna unbuckled her seatbelt. She slid out of the car, avoiding Jace's severe gaze, opened the back door, scooped the crying baby from the seat and reached over and released Matteo from his own restraint.

She held her daughter close to her shoulder, her son by the hand and wished quite irrationally that she'd had time to do something about her hair before trying to convince Jace to take them all in.

"Anna."

Jace strode over, dressed in jeans and a T-shirt that was dirty in several places. His boots were brown with dried mud and there was a smudge of something across one cheek. *His* hair, however, was perfect, slightly longer than it had been last time she'd seen him, the shaggy tips giving him a sexy, roguish look. She pursed her lips. She hated being at a disadvantage. She'd spent so many years exuding the perfect image it was difficult to allow herself to be anything less than perfect now.

"What on earth are you doing *here*?"

That was it for a greeting? No smile? No nothing? She rubbed Aurelia's back, trying to quiet her, but she knew what was wrong and standing around wasn't going to fix it.

"I know I should have called first..."

Jace frowned. "Called first? It's not like you live moments away. You've come all the way from the Island?"

Matteo had pulled his fingers away and Anna rested her hand on top of his head. Oh, the man made it sound like she was the dumbest woman in the world. Didn't he know about Stefano? Didn't he know what a shambles her life was? Was there really that much distance between them now? He made Vancouver Island sound like it was oceans away.

"I didn't have anywhere else to go. And you did say I was always welcome."

As soon as she said the words, her eyes stung sharply and her breath caught, painful and thin in her lungs. All through the trip—packing, the flight, even the drive here—she'd been fine, but now it all caught up with her. It was hopeless. She was pathetic, running away from her problems. And knowing it, tears glimmered and slipped down her cheeks.

"Anna." Jace's face softened, his eyes dark with concern. "Anna, what's happened? Don't cry. Please."

He gripped her upper arms, the fingers strong around her biceps. Suddenly it was all clear. Stefano was gone. Her father was furious. Alex was wrapped up in Melissa and their first pregnancy. She was alone, and she'd made so many mistakes, ending with the latest—coming to Jace.

"I...I..."

"Mama?" Matteo stood firm beside her left thigh, and she let her fingers trail along his dark head, attempting to allay the worry she heard in his little voice. Aurelia's crying increased.

"What's wrong with her?"

Little Matteo stepped forward from beneath his mother's hand, brown eyes blazing. "My sister is hungry and needs to be changed."

A smile twitched at the corners of Jace's mouth as he turned his attention to Matteo. He lifted his brows in a way that said he was clearly indulging the boy. "Is that right?"

Anna tried to smile, gathering herself together. Matteo was trying so hard. She hated how her son saw her sad more often than not these days. Jace was as infuriating as ever, though normally he wasn't mean about it. The friend she knew would have been teasing, or concerned. Instead he was sharp and annoyed. Maybe she'd overestimated the power of their past friendship. Jace didn't usually do things to be polite, but maybe he'd casually thrown out the offer thinking she'd never take him up on it. She hadn't thought things through. Again. Somehow she had to make it right, to convince him they should stay. "I don't want to inconvenience you, Jace. Perhaps you could point me to the guesthouse and we'll be out of the way."

"The guesthouse isn't equipped for guests. You'll have to stay at the main house. With me."

Anna was in no position to argue. Aurelia was at her limit and from the stubborn set of his chin, Matteo wasn't far behind. Right now she had to get them settled somewhere. She hadn't planned on taking over his home. The website Jace had set up for Two Willows had distinctly described the winery as having a main house and a guesthouse. It was on that basis she'd made the decision to come. Doubt flickered once more, but then Aurelia's wail pierced the air again and she knew she'd have to deal with the rest later.

"Mama, I have the bag." Matteo had gone to the car and retrieved the diaper bag, hefting it on his slim shoulders. He glared up at Jace with as much of a withering look a boy of nearly four could muster. Anna's heart smiled. Her baby boy tried to look after her as much as she looked after him. After Stefano's funeral, her father had told Matteo to watch over his mama. And here he was, bless his heart, trying to make life easier in the only way a four-year-old knew how. But it wasn't his responsibility, and it grated that her father had put the responsibility of the family on a child's shoulders—even figuratively—when it belonged squarely on her own.

But then—when had her wishes counted?

Anna lifted her nose at Jace so that he wouldn't see the glimmer of tears again. She spun away, carrying Aurelia with as much dignity as she could, considering the wails that erupted from the tiny lungs. Matteo trailed slightly behind, tipped a little sideways as he lugged along the bag. "Come, Matteo. We'll go up to the house."

It took Jace a moment to realize what was happening. Then, as he caught sight of her swaying hips, he strode forward, his jaw tight. Who did she think she was, waltzing in here and looking at him as if everything was *his* fault? He reached the door before she did and wrenched it open, the movement having little to do with chivalry and more to do with the fact that it was *his* door. And damned if she didn't sweep by him with her nose still in the air.

His sweet Anna. They'd gotten off on the wrong foot. That was all. She was used to having a nanny, and now was dealing with her children alone. He wasn't totally insensitive to what she'd been through. She'd lost her husband. And Jace hadn't even gone to the funeral. He'd heard about it from his vintner, who had heard it from a fellow vintner at a winery near Morelli's. He'd felt like a coward ever since. He'd called Alex for the details and then sent flowers. He should have known she'd be struggling. He should have offered her a place. The proud Anna he remembered would never have shown up out of the blue. She wouldn't have cried either. She'd changed, and he'd been too blind to see it.

But seeing her now was a blow to the gut. The same way it had been when he'd visited her last in the hospital, when Aurelia had been born. A reminder of what could have been. A reminder that she was untouchable. Just as she was now. This was why he stayed away. Being near her reminded him of too much. He couldn't take away the hurt of the past.

"I don't suppose you have a nursery?" She sighed with impatience and he set his teeth to keep from retorting. Aurelia's cries had quieted from screams to pitiful whimpers, and Jace suddenly saw the lines around Anna's eyes.

But Anna didn't have wrinkles. She was bright and energetic and unstoppable.

Jace wanted to help her. He'd *always* wanted to help her, even when she'd married Stefano. He'd tried to make the feelings go away but had never quite succeeded. And as much as it bothered him to have her near, he wanted to look after her now. Maybe she'd made mistakes, but clearly she was paying for them.

And yet the fact remained—he'd never really forgiven her for marrying Stefano in the first place. It had barely been three months after Jace had gone away with Alex when Anna and Stefano announced their engagement. Everything that had been was suddenly gone, like it hadn't mattered at all. Like it hadn't even *existed*. He'd been partly to blame, but she'd acted in a way he hadn't thought she was capable of. Selfish. And that fact still left a bitter taste in his mouth.

"I don't have a nursery, but there is a spare room. Up the

stairs and to the right. Down the hall you'll find a room for you and your daughter as well as one for the boy next to it." Again he saw the evidence of fatigue in her eyes. He'd seen that look of total defeat on her face before, and couldn't be responsible for it a second time. It wasn't in him to turn her away no matter what their past issues. There were years of friendship to take into account. "It's yours for as long as you need, Anna."

She looked momentarily nonplussed. "You mean you'll let us stay?"

The way she looked at him made him feel like a worm, lowly and dirty, and like she'd expected him to throw them out after one night.

"What kind of man do you think I am, Anna? Of course you can stay." He might not like it, but he'd never turn her out. He pressed his lips together. Did she really doubt him so very much?

He bent down to unlace his boots. "Give me a moment. I'll show you."

Her eyes skittered away. "That's all right, we'll find it. Thank you."

Her voice was much mollified, and he was relieved that for the moment her tears had disappeared. If only he could erase his own feelings of responsibility. If he'd been a man all those years ago instead of a coward...

He scowled as the second boot came off, and he heard her speaking softly as she led Matteo up the stairs and to their accommodations. The truth was he'd do anything to help Anna. Anna had been his family for a lot of years, always there when he needed her. He owed her.

But a poor host he was indeed, so once the boots were off, he took the steps two at a time in pursuit.

He found the three of them in the first spare room. Anna

was bent over the bed, buttoning up the front of the baby's frilly dress. Her voice was soft and musical, a change from the Anna he remembered. On the floor by the door linking the two rooms, he saw Matteo on his knees, running a toy car across the floor.

"Did you find everything all right?"

Anna's head spun around, her hands still spanning the baby's ribs. Matteo stopped the driving noises he'd been making to look up. Not in many years had Jace felt so much like an outsider.

"Yes, thank you. It's been a long day, especially for the children. They don't understand..."

Her voice broke off and he knew there was much the children didn't understand. That he didn't understand himself. He and Anna needed to talk. He needed to know the real reason why she was here. Because this was no ordinary visit, of that he was sure.

"I hope you don't mind," she continued. "We seem to have made ourselves quite at home."

"That was the intent, wasn't it?" He let a smile touch his lips, knowing they'd gotten off on the wrong foot. Her answering smile was tentative, and her eyes fell on her son.

He turned his attention to Matteo, who was watching him with openly hostile eyes. The boy was playing with a rudimentary wooden car, one Jace had made with his father when he'd been a boy and that now had a position of honor in one of the guest rooms. It was more for decoration than function these days, but he didn't have the heart to take it away from Matteo. The boy had lost enough.

"You found my car. Do you like it?"

"You can have it back. I wasn't going to hurt it."

He went over to Matteo. The boy was just old enough to

understand what had happened with his father and far too young to be able to put it in perspective. Jace squatted down in front of Matteo and tried a smile. "I made this with my dad many years ago."

"You still have toys?"

He gave Matteo a conspiratorial wink. Of course he did, only his toys now were of the faster, more expensive variety. "Certainly. You're never too old for toys."

Matteo blinked a few times. "My papa's dead. But I like my *Nonno* Roberto. He doesn't yell at me."

Jace's heart clubbed. It was all so matter of fact, and very telling. Lord, if the judgmental Roberto Morelli was being held up as an example of kindness, Stefano must have been a piece of work. What kind of life had Anna had with Stefano? And the children? Had he been a good father? Guilt piled upon guilt as Jace realized he should know the answers. If he'd been the kind of friend he should have, he would have known.

"There is a chest of toys in your room, Matteo. We will get them out of the closet. You are free to use them all."

"Thanks."

Jace smiled. With the blessing to use the toys, Matteo had lost the edge of reserve he'd been clinging to since getting out of the car, a demeanor that had seemed out of place in a boy so young.

The boy took the car and went through the door to his own room. Jace saw him take the car up onto the bed. Small boys who were yelled at. His stomach clenched. He'd had a poor childhood, but his parents had never been cruel, even when life had been cruel to them. He hoped Stefano had never been cruel to Matteo, or to Anna. Jace had enough to feel guilty about without bearing that burden as well.

He stood again and turned to face Anna. Her face was

solemn, her eyes wide. There were shadows in the depths and he wondered what had put them there. It seemed her husband's death had affected her profoundly. She was not the same vibrant woman he remembered. Children and widowhood could do that to a woman, he supposed. Had Stefano's death broken her heart?

A large tear glimmered on the baby's cheek as Anna held her in her arms. What he wanted to say and what he could say were two very different things. Saying what he thought now wouldn't help. In fact, he highly doubted he had any right to say anything at all.

"Let me know if you need anything more. I'll go downstairs and make us some dinner."

She tried a smile, but he saw the sadness behind it and fought the urge to reach out and gather her in his arms and tell her it was okay. He'd lost the right to be her defender and protector a long time ago.

"Thank you, Jace. We're very grateful for your kindness."

Kindness? The last thing he'd ever been was kind. He put his hands in his pockets and excused himself. And got out while he still could.

Chapter Two

Anna took the nipple of the bottle out of Aurelia's slack mouth. She'd fallen asleep feeding. A tiny dribble caught at the corner of her lips and Anna affectionately touched it with her finger. She'd missed out on these moments so much when Matteo had been small, and even for the first six months of Aurelia's life. She'd let Stefano steamroll her into getting a nanny so she could continue being the dutiful wife, moving in the right social circles and going back to work at Morelli's marketing department when both children had been only weeks old. He'd insisted it was expected, but she had always felt it was wrong.

Those days were gone now. She wanted to be a better mother. She wanted to be the one they looked to and depended upon. One of her biggest regrets was how she'd spent so much time away from them, leaving their care to someone else. No matter how trusted that person had been. Thinking of it now made her physically ill.

And oh, she was tired. All the travel and taking them to a new place was confusing to the children, and she was rapidly beginning to realize that when their schedules were toyed with, things did not go well. She laid Aurelia gently in her playpen and covered her with a pale yellow coverlet the color of diluted sunshine and the inside of daffodils. Tiptoeing to the edge of the room, she looked in on Matteo. He'd been very quiet, and she smiled when she saw him also asleep on his bed, his hand on a stuffed giraffe.

Her babies.

She swallowed against tears. No, no more. She would not cry, not even when she was exhausted and at her wits' end. She was done with crying. She'd done her share and was determined not to ever again. Her children deserved a happy mother, not one who leaked from her eyes at the drop of a hat. She'd made the decision to uproot them and leave the Morelli house, and she was convinced it had been the right move. She was beginning to realize there were things more important than giving them the privileges money could buy, and she couldn't stand playing the grieving widow for another moment.

She'd gone looking for a new start, a place to heal and begin again. Only four people that she was aware of knew the whole story—her father; her brother, Alessandro; his wife; and her former nanny. And that was how it would stay. She didn't want Jace to know what a fool she'd been, how her silver-spoon life had turned into a clichéd joke.

What she really wanted now was a glass of wine and something to eat. Something edible. Which meant she wouldn't be making it because her cooking skills hadn't yet caught up with her aspiring nurturing side. Their cook had shown her a few staple dishes, as had Jace's mother, but her culinary expertise was limited to those select items. Her own mother had abandoned the family when she was young.

She remembered how that felt, to lose a parent. Then she'd let Stefano neglect their children, and that knowledge kept her awake at night now. It was one of the reasons she was determined they never feel unloved ever again. She'd taken the gilded cage of marriage to Stefano when the life she'd wanted ceased to be a possibility. It had been a kneejerk reaction to a broken heart, nothing more. Her way of rebelling. Now she was paying the price. But her children never would. They were little and would forget all of this pain and uncertainty. She'd make sure of it. She had brains, means and the desire. She simply had to figure out *what next.*

She left the doors to their rooms open so she could hear if either of them woke, and left to see if there was anything she could scrounge in the kitchen.

At the bottom of the stairs she could hear movements from the front of the house, and she followed the noise and then her nose. Her stomach rumbled. She'd had a muffin in Kelowna several hours earlier, the bites fitted in between getting Matteo and Aurelia fed. But this didn't smell like dried-out muffin. It smelled like garlic. And olive oil...and something spicy. *Italiano.*

She paused inside the door.

Jace had changed out of his dirty clothes into clean jeans and a white T-shirt. She watched as his strong, dark forearms flexed as he moved the knife, slicing mushrooms and brushing them into a bowl. Jace could cook. Imagine that.

"What's cooking?"

He spun around, a supremely large knife in his hand. "You scared me."

"I'm the one who should be scared, by the size of that knife."

His lips turned up ever so slightly. "I thought you might be hungry. I know it's early, but..."

"But you'd be right. You don't have to cook for us though. I can manage."

He turned back to his chopping board. "This might come as

a surprise to you, but I like cooking."

"It does, actually." Several years ago he'd resented having to do for himself. She'd seen beyond the chip on his shoulder and had loved him anyway. It seemed that perhaps in one way, he'd relaxed his notions a bit.

He chopped more mushrooms, the rhythm of the knife firm and sure. "We didn't all grow up with cooks and maids, Anna."

She snorted. "You don't actually expect me to feel sorry for you, do you?" It was an old joke between them, the difference in their upbringings. And one made comfortably, as they both knew the other had valid claims to heartbreak.

She saw his shoulders shake a little. "You're right. That didn't really work, did it? It never did." He finished with the mushrooms and put down the knife. "The children are napping, I assume."

"Yes. Aurelia fell asleep having her bottle and Matteo was out with his arm around a giraffe."

"I'll warn you right now, I'm not good with children."

She smiled a little in response to his frown, but the smile wobbled. A bittersweet pang darted through her and she wondered if he remembered the hurtful words he'd said to her that awful day. "Oh, I don't know. You seemed to do all right once you stopped scowling at us. Toys on the premises go a long way."

She braved a look directly into his chocolate eyes. The past was over and done with. Why couldn't they leave it there?

"And I should say thank you for letting us come here unannounced. We won't stay long, Jace."

"Why not Alessandro's?" He was watching her too closely for her to be comfortable. "You and your brother were always close."

Yes, they had been. But she couldn't talk to him about this. Part of it was wrapped up in Jace, and the few times she'd mentioned it, Alex had quickly changed the subject. "I felt like I would be in the way at his place, with Melissa expecting and his own business to run. And they are building a new house, you know." Truth be told, it hurt to see their happiness, though she wouldn't say so to Alex for the world.

She halted. How did she explain what it had done to her to see her brother and Melissa? Only a few short months ago she'd been counseling him to get a move on and get married. About finding his happy ending. The ink had barely dried on their marriage certificate when her own perfect life had blown spectacularly apart.

He seemed to accept what she was saying. He turned back to the stove, lifted the lid on a pot and stirred. The scent was enough to nearly make her lightheaded.

"What are you making?"

"Risotto. I thought you might appreciate an Italian influence tonight. There's a deli down in the village that makes good sausage. Just the right spice." He moved to the fridge and took out a plate. "Here. Snack on this. You look like you're about to faint away."

The plate held an assortment of crackers, cheese and a bowl of olives in the center. Anna couldn't help it. She reached out and picked up a piece of the cheese. It was delicious.

"You made Italian?"

He gave her a bland look. "I might have issues, but I have never denied that the Italians have spectacular food."

Her lips twitched. He'd spent many an hour in the Morelli kitchen to bear that out.

"Besides, I spent a lot of time in your kitchen." He echoed her thoughts. "I paid attention. There's a cheese factory here too," he continued, leaving the topic of Morelli behind. "Really amazing feta. That's sun-dried tomato. I was pleasantly surprised to find it here."

Anna tried another sample, relieved he was keeping the topic to food and the local area. If he asked her anything personal now, she wasn't sure she wouldn't fall apart.

"Only one thing it's missing," she said softly.

Jace left the stove and came to her. Her heart beat quickly as his body nearly pressed against hers. But he only reached around her for one of the wineglasses hanging behind her head. "Perish the thought," he said in a low voice, and shivers erupted over her skin. "I opened a bottle already. One of Two Willows's. Here."

He poured her glass half-full of ruby-red liquid and handed it to her. Her fingers brushed his as she took the goblet from his hands and the wine tilted in the glass. She closed her eyes and absorbed the rich scent before taking her first, full sip of Syrah. He waited until he saw her smile of gratification before answering it with a grin of his own, and his dimple popped. Just one, on the right. Her heart tripped.

She was only reacting to Jace because her emotions were raw. And because it had suddenly occurred to her that she was staying with him without the buffer of Alessandro between them. So often it had been the three of them, all for one and one for all sort of thing. But Alex wasn't here, and suddenly it felt very intimate. It harkened back to other days when Alessandro had been abroad, studying in Italy. That month had changed everything. It had just been her and Jace left to their own devices. And with Alex out of the way, their hearts had taken over.

She stared into the swirling red liquid. "It's lovely."

"Of course it is. It's mine."

She smiled into her glass. Jace had worked hard, using his hands and smarts when he didn't have money. He'd eventually taken over the vineyard from his mentor and had renamed it as an extension of his own surname, Two Willows. As long as she'd known him he'd been driven that way. Like he always had something to prove. She'd never understood it, not really. Not until now. Now she realized how awful it was to feel like you were not good enough. Jace had always felt that way.

But that was as far as her understanding went. Anna knew something more. Success was all well and good. But she'd had it and it meant little to her now. What was important was doing right by her children. Life had suddenly become bigger. Broader, and more meaningful. And no money or accolades in the world could touch it.

She watched as he stirred hot broth into the sausage and rice mixture. He then drizzled olive oil and garlic over the mushrooms, tossed them together and then poured them into a skillet. The scent was rich and intoxicating, the sizzle of the oil and garlic hot and potent. She would never have imagined Stefano cooking in the kitchen like this. He'd demanded a cook prepare all their meals and that they be served in their formal dining room. But Jace seemed very at home with a well-equipped kitchen. The range was state of the art, the cookware heavy and high quality. It was a working kitchen, not one just for show.

No, Stefano had always taken everything like it was somehow due him. And so had she, to an extent. Being friends with Jace for most of her life had meant she'd at least realized the world didn't always work that way.

"Dare I ask about him?"

"Who?"

Jace moved to a cupboard and took out plates and cutlery. "Your husband," he replied, the word snipped as though it were a bad berry needing to be spit out.

"Ah, Stefano. I was hoping you *wouldn't* get around to asking about him."

"Why didn't you tell me?" He put down the dishes and stood with his arms folded. "Why did I have to hear it from business associates? You used to talk to me. And the news came and I heard it from my vintner. For God's sake, I had to get the details from Alex."

She swallowed, feeling slightly ill. She knew it was just nerves from talking about how her life had changed. "I didn't feel like talking to anyone, Jace. Father called Alessandro. I..." But she couldn't go on.

"I'm so sorry."

The taste of it was bitter. What would Jace think if he knew the truth? That she'd moved from loving him to being married to a man she could barely tolerate? He would hate her for sure, and she wanted to give herself a little bit of time before she had to find new accommodations. "Thank you."

His lips thinned, and for the second time she got a sense of the power behind his frame. Perhaps she hadn't seen it before because she'd known him since he was a boy. But there was no denying it. He was angry, though she couldn't quite figure out why, and it emanated from his six-foot-plus frame. All the time he'd spent hands-on in the vineyards obviously hadn't hurt either. He was strong and sun-kissed, and for a brief second it was like standing before a stranger.

A mushroom popped in the pan and their gazes broke. Jace went and turned off the burners and faced her again. The anger she'd sensed was replaced with a cool sense of resignation. That hurt more than his displeasure with her.

"Was he good to you, Anna? It's so sad that you're left now, so young. And with the children."

She'd heard it enough over the last few months that the sting should have gone out of it. But it hadn't. She didn't wince though, didn't allow herself the indulgence. This kind of misplaced pity was why she'd left Saanich and the Island in the first place.

"Don't pity me, please. I can't stand it. I've had enough of pity. I need to look forward."

"Fair enough. What are your plans?"

She had no idea. She would always have a place at Morelli, that much she knew. But she wasn't sure she wanted it. She knew she had to make a good life for herself and the children, but she had no idea how to best go about it.

"I don't have any plans. I came here to just...get my feet beneath me. To think."

"To hide."

She blinked. Perhaps she should be angry, but it was the truth. "Yes, Jace—" she sighed, "—to hide. To evaluate and make decisions away from prying eyes and useless advice."

"I see."

So did she, too late. That he was coming to the conclusion that his advice was not wanted. And perhaps it wasn't. His life was very different from hers. It was what he'd wanted, all this independence and success. He'd made the choice long ago, and to hell with the consequences. But it was the years of prior friendship that had led her here now, and so she tried to build a bridge.

"Not from you. You know me too well. I felt safe coming here."

"I'm glad." The words were soft and seemed to say so much

more, but it would do no good to try to read anything into them.

His dark gaze caught hers again and she didn't feel very safe at all. The way he was looking at her now brought back too many memories. And in the flash of a moment, she knew that if he came closer, she'd recognize his scent, his warmth, knew how his fingers would feel if he touched her.

She backed away.

His eyes cooled ever so slightly. "I *am* glad, Anna. I am glad our friendship still means something to you. That I can help in some way."

"I need to move on with my life, and forget about the past."

"You intend to forget about the father of your children?"

She wanted to lash out, whip out the words that Stefano had been a lying cheat who hadn't cared for his family one bit, but that wasn't a conversation she was up to having right now, so she merely answered, "Yes."

"Don't you care? Don't you think your children deserve to remember their father?" His face fell with incredulity.

Her blood began to simmer at the condemning tone in his words. "What do you mean? Of course I care, but what difference does it make now? He's dead."

"I don't get it." He shook his head, his eyes dark shards now. "I just don't get it."

"What don't you get? He's gone. He is not their father anymore, and he is not my husband."

"*My God!*" he exploded. "Are you really that cold hearted, Anna? Did you stop caring the moment he stopped breathing?"

Were they still talking about Stefano? Echoes of their own painful past rippled through his words. Her voice shook as she raised it in return. "Caring? I cared too much! And look where it got me. Alone! Alone and having to raise two children. And all because..."

His jaw dropped. "Because what," he said, his tone dangerously low in the quiet kitchen.

She couldn't speak for a few moments as tears clogged her throat, making it almost unbearably tight. They had never spoken of it. The day that Jace had walked away from her had been the most painful of her life. Through the years she'd put it to the side, wishing to have her old friend back, knowing it wasn't worth losing him altogether. Only that wasn't possible. The past wouldn't wash away like Matteo's chalk drawings in a spring shower. Her voice took on a raw edge of hurt. "It doesn't matter now. None of it matters anymore. What was my life is no more. That's all there is to it."

Jace took two long steps until he was before her again. He placed both of his large hands on either side of her cheeks. "How?" he demanded. "How could you have let this happen?"

He was blaming her.

She'd already blamed herself enough. But as she looked up into Jace's angry eyes, she was struck by a new truth.

Losing Stefano hadn't broken her heart. But being faced with Jace's condemnation—his disappointment—a second time just might.

Anna stepped away and out of his hands. How dare he ask such a thing? Had he no feelings for her at all?

Her voice shook as she answered him, despite how she tried to keep herself together. She wanted him to understand, but trying to say the words without letting her emotions take over proved more difficult than she'd imagined.

"Do you think I wanted this for myself? Do you think this is how I pictured my life turning out? I promise you, it's not." She took a deep breath, forcing herself to look him in the eyes and to stop wringing her hands. She'd never been that kind of woman. Not until...it didn't matter now. She'd grown up. She'd faced rejection more times than she could count and she'd always bounced back. She raised her chin. "I have left my home—the home I lived in most of my life—and have dragged my children to the back of beyond to escape the pitying looks. When I married Stefano I did not think it would end a handful of years later with me a widow bringing up two small children alone."

The kitchen echoed with silence. When Jace finally spoke, the disappointment in his voice made a weight settle in the pit of her stomach. "You were always the smart one. The cautious one. Alex and I would get into trouble and you would be sensible. And yet...of all of us, you've been the one..." He extended his hand, imploring her.

She stepped away, her chin flattened with disappointment that he should think so little of her. "The one what? Always in trouble? Always a mess for you and Alex to clean up?" The lump in her throat grew exponentially. She knew she'd failed at her marriage, and nearly as a parent. But knowing she'd somehow failed with Jace, knowing she'd let him down *again*, cut her so deeply her stomach tightened in response. She'd wanted him to understand about Stefano without her having to spell it all out. But after the day she'd had, she simply didn't have the energy to get into all the dirty little details.

"I shouldn't have come here."

His sigh was heavy as he ran a hand through his thick hair. "Where else would you have gone?"

That stung. She knew she'd been light on options but having it pointed out wasn't kind. But she'd be damned if she'd stay and let him insult her, belittle her. He understood nothing.

"I'm not destitute, Jace. I thought it would help being with a friend. I see now I should have simply escaped to one of the

Morelli properties where we could have remained unknown. And unjudged.

"I'm not judging you."

She straightened her spine. "Yes, you are. Do you really think so little of me? Is that how you see me? A screw-up who needs to have her messes fixed?"

"You were stupid to marry him." His hips came away from the counter as they faced off.

"Just consider that a fix to the mess you left behind."

As the words echoed through the kitchen, they each stepped back. Anna's heart thumped heavily. She'd crossed a line, one they'd tacitly agreed never to speak of again. She couldn't look in his eyes. She was too ashamed.

"Yes, Anna," he murmured, "you cleaned up that mess. I left you to fix it and you did."

Was that hurt in his voice? Or bitterness? She couldn't tell. She only knew the pain hadn't diminished in all the years that had passed. "I screwed up with Stefano," she admitted. Perhaps if she did that they could move past the hurtful things they had—and hadn't—just said. "I wasn't home enough, I know that now. I was selfish, and it kills me inside to admit it. If only I'd been there. It wouldn't have happened if I'd been...present in my marriage."

"What could you have done? You couldn't have prevented his accident."

"I could have prevented a lot of things."

Guilt fell heavy on her shoulders as the words hung in the air. She'd taken for granted everything would work out as it was supposed to. She'd turned a blind eye to the signs and had pretended to have the perfect life. She didn't like what that said about her. And when she'd finally gotten up the courage to do something about it, the results had been disastrous. She should have paid more attention to her marriage, rather than taking it for granted.

"Anna..." Jace opened his mouth to somehow answer her, but crying filtered down the stairs and he turned his head to the sound.

"I need to get the children," she murmured, sliding out of the kitchen and leaving him there alone.

She'd completely misread what he'd meant, he realized, pushing his fingers through his hair. He shouldn't have let her provoke him into saying things best left unsaid. She might have made the bad choices, but he'd forced her into them. Even though what she'd done had shocked him, he still found he couldn't blame her for it. What choice had he left her? And yes, he blamed her, but not the way she thought.

She wasn't responsible for Stefano's death, and this wasn't a mess of her making to clean up. Maybe Jace had made himself scarce over the years, but each time they'd crossed paths it had infuriated him to see the pompous Stefano dampen down any spark Anna had until she barely resembled the carefree woman he remembered. But she shouldn't have married Stefano in the first place. Jace had wanted so much more for her, and instead she'd let herself be swept away by a handsome face and a charming manner. All the bastard had done was to break her heart and leave her alone. It was so obvious when he looked in her eyes that she was hurting. If the man were still alive, Jace would happily make his life a living hell for what he'd done to Anna.

He'd do anything to take that pain away. It was why he'd let her stay. To prove to her that their friendship still meant something. To give her a safe place to heal. But it wasn't working out that way and he knew why.

They had too much history. A history that made nothing plain and simple. He set his jaw, took out a head of lettuce, and savagely ripped it into pieces.

Chapter Three

Anna came back to the kitchen with Matteo holding her hand and little Aurelia in the crook of her arm. Motherhood had softened her, and Jace's pulse quickened as the weight of the baby pulled her blouse taut across the fullness of her breasts. Jace turned back to the stove, hiding his reaction to her appearance.

He wasn't accustomed to these scenes of domesticity, especially not with Anna in the center of it. She'd always been so chic, so...oh, he wasn't sure. Perhaps an air of being unattainable? She'd been free and blithe and confident in herself. It was what had attracted him in the first place. Wanting something he couldn't have.

Seeing her like this—with her hair slightly messed and her makeup less than perfect, and with her babies—well, it was a completely different Anna. She was earthy and beautiful and it threw him off balance.

The reality of it was this could have been *them* if he hadn't been such a fool. Instead, he'd thrown her straight into Stefano's arms. He might not be father material, but he'd do anything to make up for his part in the whole mess. Even put up with a toddler and a baby added in for good measure.

He poured the last of the broth into the risotto and stirred, trying to block out the sound of Anna's soft voice speaking to

Matteo in Italian. The words sounded lyrical and strange, and a swell of resentment rose. It was her father, the damned stubborn Roberto Morelli, who insisted the family speak Italian as well as English. The old man had used it often enough when Jace was a boy, simply to remind him of his place and exclude him from conversations meant for family, not the help.

But Anna hadn't followed her father's example. Neither had Alex. Jace's good memories centered around them and the fun they'd had when Roberto wasn't stomping around like a puffed-up dictator.

He frowned, staring down into the pot. An hour with her and he was already feeling the old anger he'd worked hard to eradicate. He thought of his mom and dad in their little house outside Saanich. All his growing years they'd merely scraped by, never having any money for any extras or extravagances. He had seen what a toll it took on them, had seen their faces when they'd had to tell him no when he'd wanted something. He'd sworn the day he'd seen his mother cry as she counted change in her purse that he—and they—would never want for anything again. Now he supported them and himself. He had wanted more. He'd wanted to provide for his family. To be good enough for her, and Anna hadn't been able to see that. She'd called him a proud fool and had run away crying. Well, maybe he had been. But he wasn't going to be dirt under Roberto Morelli's boots. And he damn well wasn't going to be poor ever again, and neither would anyone he cared about.

"Can I help?"

Her soft voice was at his shoulder and the hair on the nape of his neck prickled. "Really, Anna, I don't mind. I cook for myself all the time." He avoided her eyes and busied himself slicing off rounds of bread.

"Jace…"

When he turned to face her, her dark eyes pleaded with his. "I...I don't want to feel like a guest." At his raised brow, she continued on. "I don't need to be pampered. I need..."

"What do you need, Anna?"

And damned if he didn't hold his breath, waiting for her answer.

"I need a place to belong. A place to be me. Or at least..." She paused again. "Oh, Jace, you've known me for years. I came here to be safe. I need a place to *find* me, and not be worried about who's going to witness it. I've been Roberto's daughter and Stefano's wife for so long I don't even remember who *I* am. If that makes any sense. I need to trust you. I know you disapprove. I'm asking you to let that go. For old times' sake."

It made more sense than she knew. His heart pounded as he realized she still trusted him after all he'd put her through, and all he'd said today. The fact she trusted him to provide that refuge staggered him. And yet, he couldn't help the feeling that there was expectation attached to it.

"Anna." He wanted to reach out and touch the creamy skin of her face, but something held him back. "My home is your home. For as long as you need. That's what families do."

He looked at the floor where Matteo shook a small toy in front of Aurelia and she giggled, showing four small teeth. "It's amazing to see you with children."

She laughed, popping the sliced bread on a sheet he'd set out and brushing the tops with oil. "Matteo's nearly four. Surely it isn't much of a shock."

But it was, for him. The day she'd stood up in church and married Stefano something had died inside him. He'd tried very hard to dig deep and be happy for her, but had never quite accomplished it. There was always something about her husband he'd never trusted. And then there were children, the final twist of the knife, and her life had moved away from his completely. He'd let it. And so had Alex. Together the two of them had failed her. He stared at the dark sweep of her hair. The least he could do was try to make up for it now.

Even if he wasn't quite prepared for children in his home. Making a meal for a beautiful woman usually involved wine and candles and soft music. Not toddlers on the floor. Candles would be a mistake, and normally he'd have music on but he'd left the stereo off because Matteo and Aurelia had been sleeping. When he'd offered them a temporary place to stay, he hadn't realized how many changes *he'd* have to make to his normal routine.

He hadn't been willing to make them years ago. His brow furrowed. He wasn't the kind to dwell on what might have been, but with Anna before him with her children, it was impossible to escape the idea.

"I haven't been as attentive as I should have been over the years," he apologized. "I'm sorry for that."

She pushed the tray of bread under the broiler and straightened. "Stefano didn't make it easy. On any of us. And you had your own life to live."

Suddenly she smiled. "You've done so well, Jace. Two Willows is getting some good buzz in the industry. Papa nearly swallowed his tongue when he saw the article on you in March." Her eyes sparkled with mischief. "And VQA designation now. That was a real bee in his bonnet."

Jace's jaw tightened. It was no secret that part of his drive to succeed was being able to rub Roberto's face in it. Maybe he'd never beat him at his own game, but he was becoming a respected member of the wine-making community. "Good," he replied shortly, moving to grate fresh parmesan into a bowl.

"But I hope you know my commitment is to Two Willows and to the wine. The other...it's just a side benefit."

"Papa means well."

He couldn't reply to that without getting in an argument with her, so he stayed quiet. After a few uncomfortable seconds, she continued, softly, "Your father must be proud."

The words caused a sting. Jace's father was laid up with arthritis, looking older than he should because of the years he'd labored too hard. Jace couldn't do anything about that. His one hesitation about building his business here rather than on Vancouver Island was that he'd have to be away from them more than he liked. His parents were determined not to move, insisting they didn't want to spend the winters amid the cold and snow of the interior. At least he knew his parents were comfortable and looked after in their home. That had been his first priority as soon as he had any profits.

For a while he'd considered going back. But setting up shop on the Island had been out of the question. Too many things had changed. Alex had moved on, and Anna had been married with children. It hurt to see them happy, his own personal brand of torture. He'd sworn when they were all children that one day he'd be like them. As secure as they had been, being brought up as Morellis. But then they'd left him behind, and he'd needed something else to fill the space inside. He'd gone from stable boy to working at a vineyard in the Okanagan, saving his money and learning absolutely everything he could. Buying Two Willows had been a good investment and a challenge. He remembered the lean times in the Willow house and didn't want his parents to have to deal with that again.

"He says he is proud," Jace replied, thinking of his dad and the last time he'd visited. "I'm able to make their life a bit more comfortable. That's the main thing."

"I know how important that is to you. But what about you? What do *you* want, Jace?"

Her eyes were earnest, large and fluid against the smoothness of her skin. He knew what he wanted right now. Beyond that he couldn't say.

At that moment Aurelia crawled across the floor and grabbed on to Jace's pant leg, gripping the fabric in her chubby fingers and pulling herself up. She bobbed there a moment, then looked up, proud and smiling from ear to ear.

"She likes you."

Jace's eyes widened as he looked down on the dark curls at his knee. He didn't move. Didn't know what to do. He'd never held a baby in his life, and he couldn't even walk to the stove because she had a death-grip on his trousers. He looked at Anna and saw her smile fade.

"I'm sorry," she murmured. "She's not quite walking and she looks for things to use to pull herself up." She bent and picked up the baby, kissing the tiny fingers as they patted her mouth.

And Jace felt out of place in his own home for the second time.

"It doesn't matter. I don't have much experience with children. I'm afraid I won't be of any help."

"You letting us stay here is help enough."

He took the bread from the oven and busied himself layering sautéed mushrooms on the tops. Help? Hah. It was a hell of a position. He'd never wanted children. She'd always known it. And he wanted to help Anna, he really did. Matteo and Aurelia were gorgeous, just like her. When he'd said they could stay, he hadn't considered he'd have a role of a stand-in father. He knew nothing about caring for small children, and he didn't much want to learn either. Keeping the winery profitable was his main priority right now. Did Anna want a place to hide out or did she want him to fill in where Stefano had failed? If she did, he resented it deeply. It was presumptuous to say the least, and he didn't want to believe it of her. Perhaps she merely expected him to make her children as welcome as she was. It wasn't as if he didn't want to. He just didn't know how. And he felt foolish admitting it.

When Jace didn't answer, Anna turned away from his frown, her heart sinking. She should have expected his reaction after all. All their lives, Jace and Alex had enjoyed the singles' scene. They were both somewhat legendary at it, in fact. Alex had only changed with the arrival of Melissa in his life. Alex was different with his niece and nephew, especially now that he and Melissa were expecting one of their own.

She settled the baby in a type of high chair she'd brought in from the car, clicking the restraints and sliding the plastic tray into place. Jace was still that man. He liked being unencumbered. She'd known it all along. He'd been very clear about his desire to remain childless back in the days when the three of them had been inseparable. She pressed a hand to her tummy. Crystal clear. It drove home the fact that as much of a refuge Two Willows provided, it was temporary. She would have to use it as a stepping stone to a brand new life for herself. It bought her time, and a reprieve to regroup. She must remember that. In some ways, nothing had changed.

She sat Matteo up at the table and gave him a slice of bread without the mushrooms on the top. She took another and broke it into little pieces, placing them on the high chair tray. Aurelia grabbed one in her fist and shoved it into her mouth. Crumbs fluttered to the floor, obvious against the dark gray of the ceramic tile. When she turned around, Jace was holding out her glass of wine, his jaw set.

"Are you quite ready?"

Anna saw the dark glint in his eyes and knew he was displeased. He'd already said he wasn't a child person. Of course he wouldn't be used to the day-to-day messes of babies. But he was making an effort. It had taken her some time to get used to it too. She met his gaze and felt her heart catch.

"I know it's more chaotic than you are used to."

"It's usually just me."

If only things could have been different. If only he hadn't been so stubborn, maybe they could have done things differently. Better. Back then, she'd have gone to the moon for him if he'd asked. But he hadn't wanted marriage and she had. He hadn't wanted children and she had. And to wish things differently would be to wish him to be different, and somehow, despite it all, she didn't want him changed.

"Thank you for the wine." Their fingers brushed again as she took the glass from his hand and a jolt skimmed down her arm into her stomach. No, she didn't want him changed at all.

"You're welcome."

He had been her ideal, and in his absence she'd settled for less than she deserved. She'd feel guilty about that for the rest of her life.

She broke the moment and went to the stove to put a scoop of risotto on a plate for Matteo and another in a bowl for her to feed to Aurelia, minus the spicy sausage. Guilt, yes, but not regret. If she hadn't married Stefano, she wouldn't have Matteo and Aurelia. And she'd never regret them. They were her one blessing. Her only remorse was that she'd taken too long to realize what perfect treasures they were. When she looked at them she saw herself and Alex and knew she could never do what their mother had done. They would never feel neglected, unloved or in the way. She would always put them first.

As she settled the children she caught the look on Jace's face. His expression was blank, like he wasn't sure what to do. He clutched a dishtowel in his hand as though awaiting disaster. Anna nearly laughed. She smiled at him. "They don't bite, Jace." Then as an afterthought she glanced at Matteo. "Much."

"Is it always this crazy?"

She bit back the irritation that simmered. Surely he didn't expect children to act like china dolls, without flaws. Jace had been a holy terror as a boy. His mother had thrown up her hands more than once and the Morelli housekeeper had once shooed him out of the house with a broom. "This is nothing. But once I know where to find things, it'll be smoother. I promise."

She put a cup of water by Matteo's plate, cautioning him to be careful. Everything was glass and breakable. She'd have to see about getting some plastic dishes so that he didn't break any of Jace's. If she'd learned anything at all, it was that accidents happened.

The look on Jace's face grew darker. She knew this was completely out of his element, but he didn't need to stand there like some disapproving saint. She straightened her shoulders. Living alone for so long had made him too rigid. Maybe he needed to have his life shaken up a bit.

She pulled a chair closer to Aurelia's and began spooning little bits of the rice mixture into the baby's mouth.

"Aren't you going to eat?"

He still hadn't moved from his spot beside the counter. Without looking at him, she fed Aurelia, mimicking opening her mouth and closing it without thinking. "I'll eat once Aurelia's through and happy. Don't wait for me."

His feet moved and she heard him getting his own plate,

then pausing by the stovetop. "I could wait. We could feed the children and then eat together."

Anna concentrated on scooping up rice on the spoon, toying with the grains as Aurelia fisted another piece of bread to her mouth. The invitation had been clear. It was an intriguing thought. Dinner with Jace. Perhaps after the children were in bed, when dusk was settling in and the day was winding down. The two of them, perhaps some candlelight and the rest of the bottle of wine. Peace and quiet and...

Resolutely, she stuck out the spoon. That was impossible. It suggested romance, and Anna was not interested in that, not by a long shot. Nor was Jace. He liked things fast and loose with no commitments, no baggage. He'd always preferred it that way. And she was a single mother. She had so much baggage at this point she didn't know what to do with it all.

He'd let her stay here as the gesture of a friend, nothing more. And she knew she'd never be the woman he wanted. Especially now. Stefano had taken a few things with him when he'd died. One of them being her pride. She was working on getting that back. But after Jace, and then Stefano, Anna was not interested in love again. It hurt too much. It hurt to have expectations of people only to have them let you down.

And she'd made a promise to herself and to her children. They would come first. They would feel wanted and loved and like they belonged. She spooned more rice into Aurelia's waiting mouth.

"I don't believe in feeding the children and getting them out of the way," she replied coldly, scraping the bottom of the bowl and building the risotto into a mound. "Maybe I serve myself last, but families sit down together. Matteo, Aurelia and me...we're a family."

Wordlessly, Jace finished filling his plate and took a seat at the head of the table. She realized belatedly that she'd just insulted him. She had deliberately excluded him when he was generous enough to offer them all a place to stay. He couldn't see that she was trying to make everything up to her babies. She'd trusted where she shouldn't have and now they were paying the price. She had to make the right choices. For once.

"I'm sorry, Jace, that was rude of me."

He looked up from his dinner, his eyes dark with what she'd swear was condemnation mixed with acceptance. "Don't worry about it. I'm used to living alone."

She pushed aside Aurelia's bowl and looked at Matteo. He was eating, but the way he held his head let her know he was also listening closely. "It's an adjustment you are making for us, and we appreciate it. I know we'll all try to respect your boundaries."

She got up and finally fixed herself a plate, though she suddenly didn't feel like eating.

This was not a family. It was a mess. She swallowed and again set her lips. But it would be a family. She'd make sure of it. It would take time. That was all.

A crash echoed through the kitchen. Jace cursed sharply and Aurelia started crying.

Anna put down her plate with a sigh and went to Matteo, who was sitting in his chair staring at the floor where water and glass mixed on the tile.

"Are you hurt?"

Jace had pushed out his chair. "He did that on purpose."

Anna sighed again. One child was enough. "Matteo. Please apologize to Jace." She said it firmly, feeling suddenly exhausted. Would she never get any relief?

"It was an accident, Mama," Matteo protested, but she

raised an eyebrow at him.

"And I told you, you needed to be careful. What do you say?"

His little lips were set in a mutinous line. "Sorry," he mumbled at Jace. Anna looked at the latter and prayed he'd just leave it for now. Thankfully, he settled back in his chair as Anna took over. She ignored the squalls from Aurelia, setting her teeth as she attended to Matteo. She picked up the large pieces of glass, laying them gently in her palm and then taking them to the sink. When she returned, she caught Matteo looking somewhat triumphant as he glared at Jace. The look Jace was returning was anything but kind, and she couldn't help but think they'd both met their match. Sometimes Matteo's stubbornness reminded her of Jace when he'd been a boy, but this time the idea didn't bring a smile. The last thing she needed was for everyone to be at odds.

And still Aurelia cried.

She sent Matteo off to his bedroom, and her annoyance grew as Jace just sat there while the baby's squeals pierced their ears. Couldn't he just go pick her up or something, or offer to clean up the mess? Instead she got the feeling he was staring at the top of her head thinking about how he knew this was a bad idea.

Children were children, and perhaps Jace needed to be reminded. After all, he had been one. And he'd been a handful. Papa had always said so.

With a cotton towel laid over the remainder of the mess, Anna pushed her hair off her face and went to get Aurelia.

"Shhh, *cara.*" She snuggled the girl against her shoulder and the tears stopped at once. "Mama's here. It's okay."

She sighed. Today she could definitely use a second set of hands. Matteo needed a talking to about attitude and Aurelia was distressed and clinging to her neck. There was glass and water on the floor and a table full of dirty dishes. Anna closed her eyes. She didn't want to inconvenience Jace any more than she already had. And in truth she'd thought they'd have privacy in a guesthouse and be completely out of his way. She wanted to do it all before he had a chance to. She needed to prove to him she was capable of handling everything.

"Leave the kitchen. I'll clean it up. I just need to get the children settled first."

"Never mind, Anna."

He refused to turn and look at her. Instead, he stood at the sink and looked out over the hill behind the house. A wave of what felt like failure swept over her. She felt like she'd let him down. Let herself down. Their first night here and all it had demonstrated was that her life was out of control.

Feeling like a failure was getting to be way too familiar.

"Please. I'm the one who caused this, let me fix it."

The words tumbled out. She did consider herself responsible and she was trying to fix things. And she kept feeling pressure to do it now, when she was really doing the very best she could. Like keeping it together was somehow expected of her. She'd always been the steady one. The one to make logical decisions rather than ones based on her heart. Not even Jace understood how much her heart had been broken back then. They thought her simply strong.

They were wrong.

"What do you need from me?" He remained staring out the window, but she heard the softening of his voice and knew he meant more than at just this moment in time.

She blinked, smelling the baby-powder scent of Aurelia mixed with the aroma of dinner.

"Understanding."

She said it softly. It settled through the kitchen like a prayer.

"Patience."

His fingers tightened on the counter's edge. She knew that request would be harder for him.

"And time. Just give me time, Jace, to make everything right."

Her neck was damp with the moisture of Aurelia's breath as Jace turned back to her. Her heart thumped heavily. What she was asking wasn't easy, or uncomplicated. Not for them. They both knew it. And yet the bond they'd forged years before held them together. And she knew he'd give her what she asked.

He came up to her, so that she had to tilt her chin to look up into his eyes, the color of rich espresso. For a shining moment, she remembered what it had been like for him to touch her. When being this close to him meant he was about to kiss her. And how his kisses had made her body sing. The memory exhilarated and frightened her.

His hand came to rest upon her cheek for a moment, and his gaze changed. Then it was gone, along with his touch as he left the room.

Chapter Four

Jace came out of the bottling shed, intending on going up to the house and sharing a cup of coffee with Anna. Instead he saw her outside, already putting the children in their car seats. A shapely backside stuck out of the rear door and his gaze clung for a moment as the skirt flirted with her slim calves. Everything in his body seemed to tighten as desire for her flared. Anna had always been couture, not a hair out of place. This more casual side of her was like a punch in the gut. Last night, with her hair curling around her temples and her cheeks flushed, she'd been more beautiful than he'd ever remembered.

It had only been a broken glass, a simple accident. But he'd been hard on the boy. He knew it and knew the sting of embarrassment. He'd been annoyed at the mess in his normally pristine kitchen, and each time he looked at Matteo and Aurelia he was reminded of how they could have been his. If only. And now she was leaving.

He'd been too hard on her yesterday too. He took long strides, nearly running to reach her side. He should have done things differently years ago. He'd tried for a long time to forget about his responsibility in how things had turned out. But he couldn't any more. Not now that she was here, with her children. Hiding from the world. A widow, for God's sake, who couldn't even bear to be in the family home. He bore more of the responsibility than he was comfortable with.

And now he'd driven her away because of his stubbornness. Again.

She opened her door and went to slide behind the wheel, and he jogged up the remainder of the dirt path, needing to reach her. Dammit, he'd promised to help her and all he'd done was snip and snarl and drive her away.

"Anna, wait!"

He braced his hands on the open door and glared. "Where do you think you're going?"

Her lips thinned and her eyes sparked. "I beg your pardon?"

"You're leaving? Just like that?"

He stood back as she slid out from behind the wheel and shut the door. "What do you mean, I'm leaving?" She angled her head as her words shot out, sharp as nails. "Do you think I'm a quitter?"

Why was it everything turned into a fight with her?

"I don't know. Are you?" He glared right back at her. Patience and understanding? Maybe he could give them to her if she waited half a minute.

"Keep your voice down. The children are in the car."

He bit back a sharp retort when he saw the look in her eyes. She was angry with him, but there was something more. A vulnerability, a weakness. Something that looked like guilt. His gaze darted from hers to the backseat and back again as realization dawned.

"You don't want them to see us arguing."

"No."

He remembered his parents arguing—loudly—as he'd grown up, but he also remembered he'd never felt insecure about it. They'd always laughed and made up. He'd never felt any fear that an argument would lead to something more permanent. Somehow last night when she'd brought the children down he'd wanted that sense of family again. He missed his parents. Missed their mealtime conversations and teasing.

But that hadn't worked out the way he'd imagined. And all the things Anna was saying—and not saying—told him her life with Stefano had been more difficult than she let on.

"Did they see you argue with Stefano?" He asked it quieter, evenly. His pulse pounded at his temple. With every passing hour it seemed he disliked the man more, if that were possible. Even if he were already dead. He'd done nothing to earn Jace's regard, either before his death or after. He had been an empty suit and all wrong for Anna, who needed someone more...

More like him. Yeah, right.

"At the end. Aurelia is only a baby, but Matteo..." Her voice faded as she turned and waggled her fingers at her son sitting in the car, pasting on a smile for his benefit. "He has big ears."

"What did he hear?"

Anna turned her head, avoiding him. He could tell by the hard line of her jaw that she was shutting him out. And damn, he deserved it, he knew that. And he wouldn't be the one to bring up the past. But at the same time, he wanted to know. Needed to know. What had Matteo heard?

"Anna."

"I don't want to get into it. Not now."

He swallowed, his throat dry with words he couldn't say. "We will talk about it later. When we're alone."

She glanced into the car again. He got the feeling she almost hoped the children would be distressed so that she could escape. The corners of his mouth twitched as he saw, as she did, Matteo lean over Aurelia's seat. He was making faces at her, and Jace heard the muffled sound of giggles.

"Why?" She asked it wearily. And he knew the exhaustion on her face was exactly why. Because she'd been hurt enough and he couldn't help her if he didn't know the entire truth.

"Because we're friends. We have always been friends, and because you trusted me enough to come here. Why do you think I was so accommodating?"

"Perhaps to prove a point? To rub my nose in it." She lifted her eyebrows, challenging.

He cursed under his breath. "No, you silly girl. I would never..." A sudden grin lit his face before he sobered once more. "All right, so maybe I would. But not this time. Not about something this important."

"Something like this?" She wet her lips with her tongue and it caught his gaze, held it for a few seconds. "What is this, exactly?"

"For God's sake, Anna. Your husband died. I know when a woman's had her heart broken."

For once, he seemed to have rendered her speechless. He took the opportunity to carry on, to attempt to make peace.

"I know things got off to a rough start. I thought I was prepared and I wasn't. I'm used to a bachelor's life. But I don't want you to go." If nothing else he'd make this much up to her. It was partly his fault things had ended up the way they had.

"It takes more than a bit of broken glass and a few dark looks to get rid of me. I thought you knew that by now."

She smiled at him. A bit of the old teasing was back in the gleam in her eyes. He'd missed that. He smiled in return. And that slow twisting happened again. The one he hadn't felt since he'd been too young and foolish to know better. When she entered a room and it was like the warmth of the afternoon sun.

He knew better now. He stepped back. Anna didn't want him. He'd once thought she did, but then she'd moved on as if what had been between them was nothing, and all the light had gone out of his days. He needed to remember that.

"Where are you going, then?"

Her hand rested on the door handle again. "It occurred to me that I could help childproof your home a bit during our stay. After last night...some plastic dishes wouldn't be amiss, and a few other items. I was just going to go into town to pick up a few things. I figured once I did that, I could talk to you about what I can do to pull my weight around here. Surely there's something you need help with."

So this wasn't about his surliness last night. He wasn't sure if he was relieved or annoyed. He might know better than to get involved with her again, but it niggled that she had gotten to him more than he'd gotten to her.

Which was stupid. Her husband had been dead only a few months. Surely the last thing she was thinking about was...

He stopped the thought in its tracks. Trying to reignite an old flame wasn't what he wanted. Anna had done enough damage when they were little more than children, turning his world first upside down and then ripping it in two. She was beautiful, no denying it, and it stood to reason that he should be attracted to her. He had been before. More than attracted. She'd been the center of his universe.

In the space of a moment, a memory surfaced. Of the two of them making love under the sun at the vineyard. The wonder they shared at being together, sharing hearts and bodies after years of being friends. Learning together.

"Good, yes. Thank you." His mind seemed unable to form

sensible words. His mouth was suddenly dry as he tried to chase the memory away. It was impossible to erase completely as his gaze was drawn to the dark cloud of her hair cascading over her shoulders, still so similar to the way it had been then. He swallowed and tried again. "Will you be back for lunch?"

She looked at him rather speculatively and he realized he sounded like an idiot. Great.

"You don't need to take care of me. I intend to do my share. I'm certainly not looking to rely on anyone."

He stepped back, relieved she was staying but off-balance by how their relationship had changed and shaken by the immediacy of the memory and his reaction to it. He'd known Anna since she had been a little girl in braids. He'd been closer to her than any other person on the planet, at one time. And now she seemed a stranger, yet not.

He'd just have to trust they could find their way to some sort of understanding.

"Why don't you take some time to rest? There's no need for you to earn your keep."

She dropped her sunglasses down over her eyes, and he didn't like how he couldn't read them any longer. "There's every reason. You don't need to look after me," she insisted.

Look after her was exactly what he wanted to do. But he sensed a fight brewing and didn't want to argue with her again. They could discuss it later.

"I'll see you later, then. Let me know if you need anything."

"I won't," she vowed and got back into the car. Before she could drive away, he turned and went into the house.

Jace was conspicuously absent when Anna returned from

town, the trunk of her car laden with items. Despite the isolation of the winery, there was something comforting in the gleam of the natural wood, the coziness of the surrounding evergreens. It was no wonder Jace had been taken with the area. Even though they were far from any big city—it would take the better part of a day to drive to Vancouver—she'd enjoyed the trip into the town.

In time past, she would have been dismayed at the lack of fine stores, but her perspective had shifted. There were things more important than boutiques. The department store here was nothing fancy, but it stocked all she needed for herself and the children. There were two bags full of gadgets for childproofing a bachelor's home. She hadn't been able to resist the ruffled swimsuit for Aurelia either, and she'd picked up a cheap plastic pail and shovel for Matteo.

Despite their upbringing thus far, the past few months had shown Anna the children cared little what things cost. They simply wanted to play and be loved. Anna knew she should have realized this much sooner. She'd felt the same way growing up. It was what had drawn her, and Alex, to Jace's family in the first place. They hadn't had material wealth like the Morellis, but there had always been boundless love. A smile and a kiss, a good-natured scolding and no one worried about spoiling precious clothing. They had each filled a need for the other—Anna and Alex's need for family and Jace's escape from poverty.

She regretted that she'd allowed family expectation to go against her better instincts. It had been the done thing to have a nanny, to attend the endless social functions, to continue to work at Morelli in marketing. That had all changed in light of Stefano's affair and the look on Matteo's face as he'd witnessed her arguing with his father. In that moment, she had taken expectation and dismissed it as she should have long ago.

Nothing was more important than her children knowing they were loved and wanted.

Matteo ran around the yard as Anna retrieved the bags and the car seat holding a sleeping Aurelia. Yes, she realized, perhaps the town wasn't the height of society, but how real was that anyway? Here people smiled and chatted, tourists and residents alike, and there was a sense of the unrushed about it.

They'd had a fast-food lunch and then made a trip to the grocery store and the market. It had taken some searching, but she'd come home with the basic ingredients for *polpettone* and *torta di mele*. She had to show Jace she didn't expect him to do anything. She wasn't a natural cook like his mother was. But there were a few things she could make passably. In her house, the cooking traditions continued even though they were second-generation immigrants. It had been the housekeeper who had taught her to make *Polpettone*.

Her purchases were rounded out by home-décor magazines. It had come to her that she could help with the abandoned guesthouse, bring it to life. Perhaps Jace hadn't thought of it, but she knew it could be an extra source of income if he'd consider opening it up to paying guests. Offer wine tours. She could put her marketing expertise to good use and indulge her artistic side with the decorating. She hoped to get some inspiration for the guesthouse within the glossy pages. Visiting the house was top of her list for the afternoon.

"Mama, can we go swimming?"

"Not now, pet." She hefted the bags, again feeling very alone. There were times that an extra set of hands would definitely come in handy.

"But..."

"I said no, Matteo. I need to put these things away and we need to visit the guesthouse. Mama needs to help Jace."

"Why?"

"Because he is being kind and letting us stay here and we do not want to take advantage of that."

But a young boy couldn't be expected to understand, and his lower lip went out. "But that's not fun. He's not fun."

She sighed, taking the steps slowly with her load. Looking at it through Matteo's eyes, she could understand where he was coming from. Jace had been cool with the children, despite his moment with Matteo and the car. So very different from the impish boy he'd been. And Matteo was mad at being caught out last night, breaking the glass on purpose.

"Maybe we can pack a bag with some snacks and toys, and you can bring them along. I think there's a back patio where you can play while I look around."

He grumbled more but under his breath, and Anna tried not to sigh. It wasn't going to be easy being mama and working and trying to do it all with a smile. At the funeral, Alex had suggested she hire some help. Her dark look had clamped his mouth shut immediately.

She would not have a nanny. Not ever again.

Aurelia woke and Anna filled a sippy cup with milk while she packed a tote for Matteo. She hooked the bag over her shoulder, settled the baby in the crook of her arm, and with her other hand held by Matteo, they crossed the lawn to the guesthouse.

It was unlocked, which was fine as it was empty and rather dirty. Matteo curled up his nose as the sunlight streaming through the windows illuminated dust motes. To the left was a large living room with a fireplace, and there were stairs directly ahead. She went through the living room to the kitchen, immediately taken with the rich, rustic wood beams throughout. It wasn't as much of a house as a large cabin, and already pictures were flooding her brain of how it would look furnished and polished and ready for guests.

A back door off the kitchen led to a small verandah, constructed of the same wide, reddish gold polished logs. The green space at the back wasn't fenced, but it was bordered by shrubs and trees that formed their own barrier, enclosing a rich green lawn. "Do you want to play here?" She looked down at Matteo, who nodded.

"Go!" Aurelia's tiny voice piped up with one of the few words she managed, probably because it rhymed with "no" and that was her favorite word at the moment. Anna put Aurelia down on the grass and dropped the tote. She took out a small pack but left the rest.

"You'll look after your sister, won't you, Matteo?"

As soon as the words were out of her mouth, she felt a longing so strong it caught in her chest. The morning her mother had gone away, she'd looked at Alex and had spoken those very words. Only Alex and Anna hadn't realized she wasn't coming back. And when they did understand, Alex had kept his promise. He'd looked after her, for as long as she'd let him.

She leaned down and kissed both children on their heads, their hair warm from the sunshine. She'd never leave her children. Never.

"I'll leave the screen open, and I'll just be inside. You call me if you need me, okay?"

"Okay, Mama."

By the time she'd reached the screen door again, Matteo had a large plastic ball out and was rolling it on the grass to Aurelia, who laughed and tried to kick it with her foot. She lost her balance and toppled onto her bottom, pushed herself up with chubby hands again and made another wobbly go at it.

They would be fine. She wanted to get started. Wouldn't it be sweet to go to Jace tonight and tell him of her plans? He would know she was down but not out. Looking forward.

She took a notepad from the pack and a measuring tape from her pocket. As she went through each room, she measured and took notes. Once it was cleaned it would be a gorgeous chalet. The kitchen was well built, and should be stocked with a full complement of cookware and dinnerware. It was a rich agricultural area, and she thought that could be played up both in the décor and in their angle. Her mind whirring, she flipped a page and started listing questions and possibilities for different types of stays and amenities provided. Her sister-in-law, Melissa, was brilliant at this sort of thing, coming from a background in the hospitality industry. She'd run it past her too.

Upstairs she discovered two large bedrooms, each with their own complete bath. One bedroom had French doors leading to a small balcony overlooking the valley, and she caught her breath at the view.

She looked down over the slope of vines, breathing in the warm air as the sight of the neat rows filled her with a sense of calm. It was beautiful, green, gorgeous, well tended. Of course, with Jace it would be. He never settled for second best. Unlike herself...

She set her lips. There was no sense thinking of that now. She couldn't change the past.

She went back inside and shut the doors, instead taking notes on renovations to the bathroom—a jetted tub would be a nice addition—and her ideas for furniture. Something sturdy, but not heavy like the current log-inspired bed. Rustic, but timeless. Satin sheets the color of Two Willows's Syrah on the bed. A fire crackling in the corner. A table with a pair of crystal glasses to the side.

She swallowed. It was so very wrong to picture herself here. With Jace. Yet here she was daydreaming, as if he hadn't already broken her heart once. She'd be foolish to let herself get sentimental over him. Maybe this had been a big mistake. She should have known seeing him like this would resurrect old longings and regrets. She should have gone somewhere else. Anywhere.

She closed her eyes against the pain that swept through her. The only thing was, she didn't want to go anywhere else. She wanted Jace. It wasn't rational and they had too much history for it not to be complicated, but deep down in her gut, she kept coming back to him. Despite the evidence, despite what she knew to be true, she also knew in her heart that Jace would provide the haven she needed right now. There was no one else she'd trust besides her brother. And Alex's words had been so cutting after Stefano's funeral that she couldn't ask him for anything.

It was just her terrible luck that she'd never quite forgotten how things had been with Jace. It was clear he was over it.

A piercing wail broke her musings and her heart jumped. Louder, more shrill and with a fine edge of panic, the screams increased and Anna ran for the stairs. Oh God. She shouldn't have left them alone in the yard while she stood here daydreaming. What had she done?

She nearly slipped on the bottom stair and grasped the railing to keep upright, only to see Jace coming through the screen door, a flailing Aurelia in his arms and a sobbing Matteo at his heels. She stopped in her tracks, completely frozen with the shock of the scene. Jace was in control yet looking quite harassed as the baby flailed and screamed.

"What happened?" She fired the question at him in Italian.

"A bee." The muscles in his arm bulged as he kept a firm grip on Aurelia, using the other one to wet a cloth he found in a drawer. He pressed the cold cloth against the baby's arm. Anna rushed forward to examine the spot. It was red and swelling.

"I got the stinger out."

Anna took Aurelia into her arms, but the baby didn't seem to care who was holding her. Her cries continued.

"I should have been with her." She felt the weight of it heavy upon her. Why was it she seemed to fail at everything these days?

"It probably would have happened anyway. Don't be too hard on yourself."

Anna looked down at Aurelia's arm. It was beginning to swell. Jace looked too. "Does she have allergies?"

Anna's gaze darted to him in alarm. "I have no idea. Should we have her checked?"

Ever so calmly, Jace examined the tiny arm. "I don't think so. The only swelling is at the site. Of course a pharmacist would know better."

Matteo's voice sounded particularly small, devoid of the bravado he'd been demonstrating of late.

"I'm sorry, Mama. The bee came and she slapped at it."

"It's not your fault, Matteo."

Two fat tears sat on the boy's cheeks. Jace sighed. "I can run to the pharmacy if you like."

Anna looked up at him over the whimpers of the child in her arms. His talk of allergic reactions struck more fear in her than she was prepared for. She didn't know what she'd do here alone if anything happened. And she hated feeling dependent on him. Why couldn't things just be simple for a while?

"We could...come with you."

A muscle ticked in his jaw as he took the cloth and re-wet it. He folded it carefully and placed it over the spot once more.

"We'll have to take your car, then."

She stared at him stupidly. "We will?"

"The Porsche won't handle baby seats."

She blushed. Of course. Nothing stated bachelorhood any stronger than a two-seater rocket with three hundred and fifty-five horsepower. There was a time long ago that such an obvious display of hubris wouldn't have bothered her. Now it just accentuated how different their lives had become. How changed their priorities were.

"Never mind. You must have things to do. You didn't invite me here to be more trouble. I can drive us in."

"Anna, you're in no shape to do that. Besides, you'll have one eye on Aurelia all the time and you can't drive safely that way."

She laughed a little, the sound dry. "You're worried about safety when you drive that?" She gestured towards the parking pad with her chin.

"I'm not driving children around, am I?"

Her bubble deflated.

"Let me take you."

"Fine." She swept past him, carrying the diaper bag.

The drive to town was quiet except for Aurelia's whimpers. Anna was relatively sure now that the baby was fine, but the spot was still puffy and red. The pharmacist gave them some cream and an antihistamine to counteract the sting.

The drive home was different.

In the moments when Aurelia had been wailing, they'd worked as a team. Now that it was over Anna could step back and evaluate what had happened. She realized a few things.

The first being that Jace had simply reacted and treated Aurelia most efficiently. He'd scooped her up, taken out the stinger and had put a cold cloth on it to soothe. He'd done what she should have and that burned.

But he'd done more than that. Seeing him holding her daughter in his strong arm had done something to her. It had broken something she'd thought healed a long time ago. It made her wish. It made her wish that her children were his and not Stefano's, and she resented him for it. He'd had his opportunity and he'd turned away from her and their chance at happiness. He'd dutifully taken up the position of friend, and she'd accepted it rather than settling for nothing at all. But seeing him with her daughter on his arm pierced her heart in a way she hadn't thought possible.

"Maybe it would be better if I took the children and went to Alex's." She murmured it but Jace got the message.

"Because of today? Bee stings happen."

She couldn't tell him the real reason why, because she never wanted him to know how deeply her feelings ran.

"Why were you at the guesthouse in the first place?" he asked, looking at her briefly, then turning his attention back to the winding road.

It was as good an opening as any. It was the only thing she could think of at the moment to balance things out. A way to escape the feeling that he was taking over, or that she was starting to rely on him. She didn't want to rely on anyone. She merely wanted a place for some peace so she could figure out what she was going to do next. Perhaps now was the time to draw that line in the sand.

"I had an idea this morning. That guesthouse is sitting empty, which is a shame. Look at what you've got here. A gorgeous, secluded winery on the river, minutes from the

Shuswap. This is a tourist trap in the summer. Why not fix up the guesthouse and rent it out? Either by the night or week. And you could do wine tours. I picked up a local events paper today and a few other wineries in the area have them."

"And who do you suppose would run it?"

"That's what you hire people for."

"People like you?"

She paused. What an interesting thought. A fleeting vision of herself playing hostess while Jace ran the vineyard and the children played on the grass...but no, it was pure fantasy. This was temporary, not a permanent relocation. "Of course not. I have a job with Morelli. But I can help you get it ready, get you set up. It's what I do best."

"Go on."

"I have Morelli contacts and a good eye, and you know it." She hesitated, took a breath, and delivered what she figured would be most important to him. "It would be an extra source of income for the winery while you're still growing your production numbers."

Jace considered Anna's proposal. It was an interesting idea and not a new one. He'd thought of it already, but with taking over the winery and trying to maximize the grapes he already had, there'd been no time to explore it. He already knew he needed to get the store operational again, to sell his wines on-site. He wanted to do tours and promote Two Willows wines right on the premises. If the guesthouse could make money, he could pay one person to do both.

"How would your father feel about you using Morelli contacts to help me? I'm the competition."

As soon as the words were out of his mouth, it was like he

could hear Roberto's response in his head. Two Willows? Competition? Hah. Roberto Morelli would never consider Jace his equal, and he knew it. So did Anna.

Anna looked away and out the window as she answered. "He doesn't need to know."

Silence reigned for a few minutes.

"How long?" He surprised himself by asking it, by even considering it. It meant Anna here, within reach but completely out of reach, for an extended period of time. It meant the children underfoot too.

"Not long. It would depend on shipping times for furniture and fabrics, but the house is already lovely. It just needs...some Morelli refinement."

The sound of a gentle baby's snore came from the back and he couldn't help it, he smiled at her just a little. Didn't Anna know he couldn't refuse her anything? He blustered and carried on, but when she looked at him like she was now—soft and expectant—he was done for. He always had been.

He pulled into the drive at Two Willows and stopped, parking next to the Porsche. A quick glance in the back told him both children were asleep, worn out from their day. He held out his hand to Anna. "Then you have a deal, Ms. Morelli."

In the moment, he'd forgotten she wasn't Ms. Morelli anymore, but she didn't correct him. Instead she placed her hand in his, the grip firm but the skin soft as silk. "Deal."

Before he could change his mind, he leaned over and pressed his mouth to hers. Her soft lips opened beneath his, surprising him. She tasted like strawberry gloss, and memory slammed into him.

What had he done?

Her lips parted from his but she remained just a breath

away. When he opened his eyes he saw her lashes still lay on the crests of her cheekbones.

His angel. She always had been and he'd just been careless.

"I'm sorry," he whispered.

Her eyes opened, but they weren't dreamy like he'd expected. Like he was feeling. They were dark and condemning.

"Me too," she replied, and leaned away to get out of the car.

Chapter Five

Aurelia was put down for a nap between the pillows again and Matteo watched a DVD while munching on the goldfish crackers he'd picked out at the store. Jace had disappeared to the bottling shed once more after they'd arrived back at Two Willows and Anna took her frustration out on her *polpettone*.

She added ingredients to the meat, took off her rings, and kneaded it all together in the bowl with her hands, the muscles in her slim forearms cording with each push and roll. When she'd come here, her only thought had been a desperate need to escape from the pitying looks and her father's endless edicts. Anna had considered that her history with Jace might create a problem, but she'd told herself she would keep it firmly in the past as she moved forward. She hadn't considered those feelings would rise up again with such force. All the things she'd wanted back then were still in her heart. And seeing Jace with her baby in his arms brought it all crashing forward. Then he'd gone and kissed her.

She bit down on her lower lip, still tasting him there. No. It was impossible.

She didn't know what had possessed him and she'd been unable to utter a single word after she'd gotten out of the car. There was too much to say and so she'd been unable to say anything at all.

She formed the meat into a rectangle and put it in a pan, then washed her hands before sliding the dish into the oven to bake. If wishes were horses and all that. A family wasn't what Jace had wanted then and it still wasn't. She only had to look around this place to see that. So why had he kissed her? Especially now, when she was a widow with two small children he'd never wanted? Was he playing with her feelings? She didn't want to believe it. But what else was she supposed to think? He had to know she wouldn't take such a thing lightly.

Maybe she should. It was only a kiss after all.

But there wasn't such a thing as *just a kiss* with Jace. She sighed. Maybe she should just go back to the Island. She still had her job and the house.

But the very thought made her stomach curl with anxiety. Her father with his long looks and pronouncements. Stefano's family. Stefano's *mistress*. And all the whispers behind the hands of their friends and associates. All the sympathetic faces and words of condolence about a senseless tragedy when none of them knew the truth. She picked up a peeler and began viciously peeling potatoes. No, she couldn't face that again. She didn't know what her life was, or what it would become, but she knew it wasn't *that*.

The door opened and shut and she held her breath. What could she say to Jace now? She didn't want to talk about the kiss, and she didn't want to talk about *that day*, the one single day in her life that had changed everything. She definitely didn't want to talk about Stefano. Yet they couldn't continue on for long the way they were.

"You're cooking?"

She tried a smile. "It's been known to happen a time or two."

His face relaxed slightly. "You have people for that," he

teased.

"My father has people," she corrected. She held out an olive branch. "I thought I'd make *polpettone.*"

"No one makes *polpettone* like..." Eagerly he went to the oven and opened the door a crack, eyeing the Italian version of meatloaf.

"Francesca." She named the cook the Morellis had employed while she and Alex were growing up. "I know. It's her recipe."

"It is?" He shut the oven door and straightened, staring at her hard.

"I did stay in touch with her, you know, after she retired. She gave me her recipe. Also showed me her secret to potato puree."

"You surprise me."

The words warmed her. It was nice that for once she wasn't completely predictable. "I'll take that as a compliment. Though I can't guarantee it will taste like hers. I would never presume to aspire to such heights."

He wiggled his eyebrows. "I often ate it cold."

"Yes, you always claimed it was better the second day."

He smiled as the memory drew them together. It was a genuine smile, and her heart caught.

"Jace," she began, putting down the potato and drying her hands on a towel. She desperately wanted to put things back on a practical footing. "I'm sorry we've put you in this position. I was feeling so stifled that I needed to get away, and I just descended on you without warning. I think...I think I was afraid you'd say no if I asked first. I'm glad you've decided to let me repay you by helping with the guesthouse."

The kitchen was quiet, only the distant sounds of the

television marring the perfect peace.

"It is very hard to say no to you." The admission was soft and telling.

"It wasn't always." The answer came automatically and she wanted to cut out her tongue. What had happened to making sure they didn't talk about their past relationship?

"It means a lot to me that you felt you could come to me. I know I've been difficult the last twenty-four hours."

"Who wouldn't be? We took you completely by surprise."

"Yes, you did. I wasn't prepared. I wasn't prepared for children. But I didn't mean you weren't welcome."

She bit down on her lip. Not welcome was exactly how she'd felt. Until the moment their mouths had touched. Then it had felt very, very welcoming.

"About what happened in the car..."

He cleared his throat. "I'm sorry. I wasn't thinking. Your idea for the guesthouse is a good one. I got carried away, that's all."

It was what she'd wanted to hear and yet it still deflated her. But now, like then, she preferred keeping the friendship between them. The friendship was what would sustain them. She had to focus on that.

"We go back a long way, don't we?"

"Yes, Anna, we do. I'm so sorry I wasn't there for you."

She swallowed heavily. It had been years since she'd heard him speak her name in just *that* way, and warmth curled through her insides. Did he have any idea how much she'd missed him over the years? How she'd needed him only to have him treat her like she was his best friend's baby sister?

"I could have used you on my side."

She lifted her eyes and lost herself in the regret she saw

reflected back to her. "I let you down," he admitted. "It's not something I like about myself."

How could she answer without getting embroiled in the one topic they never discussed? She chose her words carefully. "You were honest. I understood why you kept away."

For moments their eyes clung. Questions hovered on Anna's lips, but she was too afraid to hear the answers so remained silent. She begged him to forgive her with her eyes. Hoping he understood without words what it was she wanted to say.

"I'm here now," he said gently. "And I hope I'm not too late."

He came forward then and put his arms around her, enfolding her in a hug. She closed her eyes as her head rested against the inside of his shoulder. Her arms curved around his back and she held on, drawing strength from him. He felt so good. He hadn't held her for many years, and it took her back to the rolling green hills of the Morelli estate. The feelings rushed through her and she tried to ignore most of them and concentrate on what she really needed right now. Strength and support. Her champion back. Even if they were both more than a little flawed.

She pushed away a little, feeling better but still realizing he deserved to know the truth about Stefano's death. It wasn't fair to keep it from him any longer. There had to be some measure of trust, of honesty between them. Despite their fights, they'd built bridges the last few days. He had to hear it from her.

"I need to tell you about Stefano, and what brought me to Two Willows."

"I am sorry about your husband. I can't imagine how you must feel. Of course you would want to get away from reminders of him."

His chocolaty eyes held her motionless and she knew she

had to explain. It was as good an opening as any to tell him how things had really been. It wasn't fair for her to let him go on thinking she'd had a perfect marriage. Or that she was nursing a broken heart. And if he thought less of her in the end, so be it.

"They aren't the kind of reminders you think. I certainly didn't run because of a broken heart. I ran because being home made me feel like an imposter. All the looks and words made me feel guilty for not grieving more. Oh, Jace, I couldn't breathe."

"You did love your husband, didn't you?"

It was a question for which she had no clear answer. She had to keep her hands busy. She gave him a pot and the two potatoes she'd already peeled, so he could wash them. She picked up another and began peeling. He worked beside her without a word of protest, somehow understanding that in the difficulty she had to keep occupied.

"I did, but not as I should have. I loved him for *what* he was at first. Then I found out *who* he was and I hated him."

"I don't understand."

She handed over another potato.

"Stefano was a wonderful catch on paper. My father knew it. I knew it. So did Stefano. He was from a good family, an Italian family, and that was important to Papa."

"I remember." The bitterness bled through Jace's voice. Roberto Morelli had looked down his nose at Jace's family. Mike Willow had looked after Morelli's stables, an expensive hobby of Roberto's that made him look good. Jace had worked part-time there as soon as he was old enough. Roberto hated that Alex and Anna were friends with someone so beneath them.

But Alex and Anna weren't such snobs as children. Jace had spent hours with them, roaming the vineyard, sneaking into the kitchen, playing in the stables. All the places where Roberto wasn't. Jace had never truly felt the difference between them until he'd come back and found Anna engaged to Stefano.

"Please," she begged him softly. "You have to understand. Papa was very...persuasive. Stefano had money and security. We had a perfect life and in my way I thought I loved him. But I did it with my head, and not my heart. And my head was very, very wrong. It was more of an alliance than a marriage. He'd wanted a connection with Morelli."

"And you wanted..."

The air seemed to still all around them. What had she wanted? She'd given up on love and happy ever afters. Everything she'd wanted had crumbled around her. She'd hardly cared. Stefano had seemed as good an idea as any. He had been older, and charming and attentive at first. And in a way it had been her final act of defiance. She'd wanted to hurt Jace the way he'd hurt her. Only she'd ended up being the one hurt in the end. Jace had come through without a scratch.

Now he seemed to be holding his breath, waiting for an answer. For some odd reason she almost felt like she was being tested. But why, she couldn't comprehend. When she'd met Stefano, she and Jace had been over. Alex had gone to Kelowna to study another wine operation and he'd taken Jace with him. They stayed nearly two months, while she'd been alone, heartbroken and angry.

"I don't know what I wanted. I thought he would give me a comfortable life. And for a while he did. Then I found out he was having an affair with our nanny just after Alex and Melissa were married."

The potato dropped, unwashed, into the pot, and Jace turned a quarter turn. She could feel him staring at her profile but she didn't dare look up.

"What did you do?"

"We didn't have a great love affair, Stefano and me. It was...it was understood that it was based greatly on appearances. But the one thing I refused to tolerate was infidelity. He never even attempted to deny it. Nor did he take any great steps to hide it. Honestly, I think my pride could have taken it if it had been anyone other than the woman I entrusted with my children. I confronted him with it."

The peeler scraped at the potato furiously. "I demanded he stop. He wondered why he should. Then he asked what I was going to do about it."

"Good for you. What did you say?"

"I didn't have an answer. I guess I thought being caught would be enough. But no. So in the end I threatened to divorce him."

Jace's braced his hands on the edge of the counter as he let out his breath in a whoosh. She could sense his shock. Divorce wasn't something taken lightly and she couldn't escape the feeling that her answer disappointed him as well. He was going to think even less of her, if that were possible. She blinked, determined to get through to the end so she could get it over with once and for all.

"I know," Anna continued weakly. "He laughed at me. He came right out and asked what I thought my father would say to that. Papa clings pretty tightly to what he calls 'the old ways'. But Stefano took it too lightly. It made me mad. I swore to him I'd end our marriage if it was the last thing I did."

"And Roberto? What did he say?"

The hurts piled on top of one another, weighing Anna down. "He expressly forbade it. No daughter of his would disgrace the family with divorce." Finally, she put down vegetable and peeler. She stared out the window. This was what her charmed life had become. Away from the home she'd known and loved, away from the people and places that were familiar just to escape her own guilt. "I couldn't stay at Morelli, so I stayed in our house and contacted a lawyer."

Jace cursed. "Damn your father and his narrow mindedness. What kind of man would turn his daughter away?"

Anna couldn't help but smile a little as her heart warmed. This was why she'd come to Jace. Despite their past, she knew deep down he'd be on her side. "I really didn't expect anything else, Jace. Anyway when Stefano found out I'd hired a lawyer, he took his mistress—the nanny who had rocked my children to sleep, supposedly loved them—on a trip on the sailboat. He was arrogant and complacent. And wooing her with Morelli's finest, it would seem."

She tried to keep the loathing out of her voice, flattening it to calm the awful emotions churning inside her. "There was an accident, and he died. We just kept the mistress part quiet, and everyone considered it a horrible tragedy. If people knew, they said nothing to me about it. Only me, Papa and Alex knew the marriage was already ending. But it is hard to keep it a secret that she was there with him. She went into hysterics with the coast guard."

"Bastard." Jace spit out the word and spun her around, his hands firm on her shoulders. "And now what, you feel guilty?" His gaze burrowed into hers. "You feel responsible?"

"Yes, yes, I do," she answered quietly. She eyed the pot of potatoes, most of which were unrinsed. She reached over, took it off the counter and ran it under the water. Anything to keep her hands busy. They wanted to reach over and grip his, to find strength in his fingers, but she knew she couldn't rely on that too much. "I didn't create the storm, but when it comes right down to it, I was the one who provoked him. I was the one who hadn't been attentive enough, hadn't seen the signs. And yet I couldn't stand the sight of him, knowing what he'd done. You must understand, never would I have wished him dead. *Never.* But playing the sorrowful widow, knowing what I knew, was impossible. I couldn't take it another minute. And that's why I'm here. I'm not here to recover from some broken heart. I'm here because I have to find a way to face up to all the mistakes I made."

Jace was gutted. Of all the things he'd imagined, this wasn't it. He'd resented her perfect life for so long it was a shock to realize it hadn't been perfect at all. Tension rippled through him. He wasn't sure what he felt at this moment.

Responsible? Yes. He'd felt responsible all these years, feeling like he'd pushed Anna into Stefano's arms. If only he'd handled things differently. If he hadn't taken the coward's route out. It didn't matter that he'd been young. Or that he'd loved her more than he thought possible. It had become too much for him to handle, and instead of dealing with it he'd run away and left her alone.

Anger? Absolutely. At her, for making the choices she had. At Stefano, for being such a failure as a man and a husband. At himself for neglecting their friendship as long as he had, and for not seeing what was happening right beneath his nose. Why hadn't Alex or their father done anything about it? They'd all failed her. But especially him.

And disappointment. Beneath all the other feelings was a heaviness that he recognized as disappointment. Anna had been his ideal back then. A girl who didn't make mistakes. She was everything he wasn't. Privileged, beautiful, classy. Smart, serious, level-headed. He'd liked those things about her. He'd gone to Kelowna with Alex needing space, but knowing when he returned they would figure everything out.

And on the night he returned, it had been her engagement party to Stefano. Everything he'd known to be true about Anna dissolved in that moment when he'd realized she was marrying someone else.

Now it had all come to a head with this—Stefano dead, Anna left behind with two children. Children that might have been his had things been different.

He realized he'd been standing in the same place for a long time. Anna put the pot of potatoes on the range, and he saw her brush her fingers across her cheeks when she thought he wasn't looking.

He wanted to console her. Yet at the same time all the other resentments were so close to the surface he didn't know how. Or even if he should.

"You are not the only one who made mistakes."

"I don't want to talk about it anymore, Jace. I came here not necessarily to forget, but to look forward instead of backwards to things I can't change now."

Oh, that burned. He wondered what sorts of things she'd change. If her regrets even went back as far as his.

"And looking forward means what?"

She straightened her shoulders. Moisture still clung to her sooty lashes and he wanted to reach out and touch them with his finger. He didn't. With each passing hour, her being here went deeper than a debt to an old friendship. Now he wanted answers. Now he wanted to know if everything from back then was true. Or if it had been a girl's fantasy.

"It means finding the best life for my children. They deserve more than I've given them. They are my priority, first and last."

He pressed his tongue against his teeth. It was no girl

standing before him now, but a beautiful woman, a mother. Longing warred with hatred and he closed his eyes, taking a breath to steady his nerves. She had changed, grown. Why couldn't she have thought this way when they were younger? Why had she been rash and hurtful? She'd destroyed his world so very casually, ending it all with a wink and a bright smile the day of her party with Stefano. It had been years and the slash of pain had tempered to a dull ache. But now, with the flush and bloom of motherhood plain to see, the knife's blade sharpened again.

The thought raced through his mind unbidden: *It should have been me.*

"Jace?"

She came forward and put a hand on his arm. He stared down at her fingers. It wasn't so long ago they would have been manicured and polished. Now they were smooth, soft, unadorned.

He reached down and removed her hand from his arm.

"Call me when dinner's ready, will you?" He heard clipped tones in his voice but didn't care. "I have to do something."

It was a paltry excuse and he knew it. It had been easier thinking she'd loved Stefano and was grieving. Now he felt adrift, not knowing anymore what was true and what wasn't, and wondering how on earth to find out without getting in too deeply himself.

Jace took himself down to the vineyard. Normally walking through the rows of vines comforted him, but not today. Today he was restless and soon found himself at the edge of the water at the place where the winery had acquired its name—the curving bend of the river, marked by an ancient willow, the feathery curtains of branches lending an air of calm dignity to the jut of land. He'd stepped on to this property, seen the lone tree standing guard and had just known. He belonged here.

An old wooden dock traversed out several feet, and he supposed in years past perhaps rowboats or kayaks had called it home. He thought of Matteo and the look on the boy's face when he'd claimed he hadn't hurt Jace's toy car. He wasn't one for children, but the innocent statement had affected him more than he'd realized at first. What sort of life had he had with Stefano? Had he been afraid of his father? Constantly trying to please him? What would it have been like if he had been theirs, his and Anna's?

It was no good to think about it. Jace knew if Matteo had been theirs, life would be very different. Jace would have found himself under Roberto Morelli's thumb. Perhaps he did owe the old man something after all. His disdain for Jace and his father had allowed Jace to become the man he was today—answerable to himself and no one else. He'd built the life he'd wanted all along.

Matteo's eyes seemed to follow him everywhere. It had to be difficult, losing a father and then moving away from the only home he'd known. He should bring the children down here to swim. Or get a little boat to row around, something safe that they could all sit in and enjoy the area around the winery. The current here at the curve where it pooled wasn't strong.

He ran a hand through his hair. This was stupid. What was between he and Anna was long over. She'd made her choice. Second-guessing and living in the past, this wondering what if...it wasn't like him. Anna brought back memories and old feelings. It was that simple. Jace just had to move past it. The answers he'd craved earlier didn't matter. They would not change what was done. What she'd done.

He made his way back up the slope to the house. As he drew closer, he saw the door open and Anna come out onto the verandah. He could tell when she saw him because she stilled. It was odd to think of someone being up there waiting for him, and when she offered a weak smile at his approach, he knew they had to move past this afternoon. Somehow.

"Dinner's ready?"

"It is. I just put the children at the table."

He followed her in, disappeared momentarily to wash his hands, and then entered the kitchen.

The dining nook was transformed. Stubby candles burned at the center of the table, the scent of wax and vanilla mixing with the delicious smells of dinner. Their places were set, and there was not the mess there had been last night. Matteo's hair was freshly combed and his clothes straightened. He ate from a melamine plate and drank milk from a plastic cup. Aurelia sat in her chair, the tray holding a bowl with creamy potatoes, mashed vegetables, and tiny bits of *polpettone*. She smiled a toothy smile up at Jace and banged a covered cup against the tray, swinging a plastic spoon with the opposite hand. A *torta* sat on the marble countertop, and Anna was pouring wine from a bottle into two glasses.

It was the kind of domestic picture he had never expected to see in his house.

He did not know what to say to Anna.

She handed him a glass of wine. "Sit down, Jace. Please."

He did. And grew even more uncomfortable as she served him a plate.

"Thank you."

"You are welcome."

The stilted words were fraught with things unsaid. Jace

instead looked across the table at Matteo. "Do you like to swim, Matteo?"

The little boy speared a piece of meatloaf and popped it in his mouth, eyed Jace warily and nodded, his nearly black hair flopping on his forehead.

"I was just down at the water. Perhaps you'd like to go sometime."

Belatedly he looked up at Anna. "Does he have a swimsuit?"

"He does."

"And Aurelia too?"

"She's a little young for the water."

Jace made the motions of eating. "Not if she were in your arms. It can get very hot here. The humidity can be quite something, and the river is refreshing."

He tried not to think of Anna in a swimsuit. Hers would be something unbearably chic, probably two pieces, and her long legs...

He cut into his meatloaf.

"My papa didn't like swimming."

He looked up. Matteo had started shaping his potato puree into an odd-shaped mound. "No?"

"No. He liked his boat. It was a big boat. It had huge sails." Matteo spread his arms wide, demonstrating.

"I bet that was fun."

Matteo looked up. "I saw it in a picture."

Jace blinked. "Oh."

"My papa drowned, did you know?"

It was like a blow to the solar plexus, the kind that makes a hollow echo and drives all the air from the chest. Matteo was

Donna Alward

barely four. And he talked of his father's death like one would say, "We went to the store, did you know?" Did he understand the magnitude of what had happened? Or would it be forgotten?

"Matteo."

Anna's soft admonition washed over them all except Aurelia, who was sucking potato off her fingers. Jace looked over at Anna and noticed how her hair curled up in wisps at the ends, the shade of rich mink. Irrationally, he could only think of losing his hands in the heavy mass, as her soft voice sighed against him. His gaze captured hers and her hand fell still, halfway to her mouth.

Matteo's puree was taking on the shape of a mountain as he carried on the conversation, oblivious to the silvery something shimmering between Jace and Anna. "What, Mama?"

She dragged her gaze away from his, looking at her son instead. "Eat your dinner and stop playing please."

Quiet ensued for a few moments. Jace was reminded of home. The *polpettone* was indeed very much like Francesca's, and Anna had made a salad of fresh spinach and avocado. The one good thing about the "big house" on the Morelli estate was the food. He'd gained a whole new appreciation for Italian cooking from the leftovers alone.

"Do you have a boat, Jace?" Matteo piped up, disturbing the silence. "I wanted to go on Papa's boat and he wouldn't let me."

For the briefest of moments, Jace remembered being on the outside looking in. He remembered wanting so badly to have the things others had and knowing it was impossible. Of begging his father for them when he was too young to understand the financial constraints of his family.

His demanding questions must have hurt his parents to answer. To have to constantly remind Jace they didn't have the money for whatever it was he wanted. He had always only remembered what it had felt like to receive those answers.

But now, at this moment, faced with Matteo's pleading eyes, he thought he knew a tiny bit what it must have been like for his parents. Even though Matteo wasn't his, he was glad his financial circumstances meant he could answer differently than his father had.

"I should, shouldn't I? Of course, with this little river, a sailboat like your papa's is out of the question. But I've been thinking about getting something smaller. Would you like to go shopping for one?"

He saw Anna's lips drop open out of the corner of his eye, but he kept his gaze on Matteo.

"What do you say? Do you want to help me pick one out?"

Matteo's hair flopped again against his forehead, and Jace cut into his dinner with renewed gusto.

Someone had to spend time with the boy, other than pressing him into being a playmate for his sister or toting a diaper bag. He needed someone who understood what it was to be a boy. Jace scooped up a forkful of potato with satisfaction.

Matteo would not be excluded. Jace would make sure of it.

Chapter Six

Three days later, Jace carved out an afternoon and made good on his promise to Matteo. Anna was surprised when he made the announcement over lunch. While she stayed with Aurelia, the two "boys" went to a local dealer, shopping for a small motorboat they could use to zoom up and down the river. He took Anna's car in deference to her insistence that Matteo ride in the backseat, properly fastened in his booster seat. Anna spent an hour at the guesthouse taking notes, and then took Aurelia back to her room for a nap in her new playpen.

Anna stared down at the sleeping baby. She supposed she should get a crib. Right now, Aurelia's lashes lay against her cheeks and her hands were fisted, lying on either side of her head the way babies do. Her angel. So far she'd let the warmth of the little body comfort her in the large bed, taking away some of the loneliness, reminding her of how deeply she loved her children. But she couldn't sleep with Aurelia forever. The playpen would do for naps but that was all. A crib seemed so permanent though, and they wouldn't be at Two Willows that long. Anna tiptoed from the room, shut the door partially and eased her way downstairs in the silent house. The bed could wait until she figured out a more permanent situation for them all. A place where they could truly settle. A home.

She blinked back the stinging in her eyes. Occasionally it

hit her that she was the head of her own little family now. It was a hollow feeling, lonely and isolated, and filled with awesome responsibility.

But for now she had a guesthouse to renovate. She spent an hour making decisions and phone calls, asking for quotes, placing orders and booking painters. When it was done, she tied a scarf over her hair, found a dusting cloth and polish in the broom closet and began polishing the furniture.

When Jace and Matteo arrived home, she was mopping the kitchen floor.

"Mama, Mama, we got a boat!"

She put her mop back in the bucket and stood, placing a hand against the small ache at the base of her spine. "You did? What color is it?"

"White. With red stripes!"

"Hold on, young man." She put an arm out to stop his progress. "Take off your shoes and stay out of the kitchen. I'm scrubbing."

Matteo paused and pushed his shoes off with his toes.

Jace followed Matteo in the house.

"What on earth are you doing?"

She smiled brilliantly. "I'm cleaning." But Jace's scowl faded the smile from her lips. "What?" she asked, tilting her head.

"You don't have to clean my house."

She stared at him. "I know I don't have to. Aurelia is sleeping. I am waiting to hear back on some quotes. And once I started—"

"Just stop. Put those things away. The cleaning lady comes tomorrow."

What was his problem? Anna's brow wrinkled and Matteo

looked from her to Jace and back again. Granted, she had grown up with a housekeeper and cook, and had kept the same when she'd been married to Stefano. But it didn't mean she didn't know how to clean.

"Then she can have a day off, can't she." She kept her grip firmly on the handle of the mop.

"You are not to clean my house."

Her chin flattened at his outburst. Fine. If he didn't want her touching his things, she wouldn't. She let go of the mop, caring little that water splashed over the tile.

"You're insufferable."

"You are a guest here, Anna. Not a maid." He made a slashing motion with his hand.

She put her hands on her hips. Matteo had disappeared back out the door but she'd go after him in a minute. "I never said I was a maid. I was simply trying to help out while you were gone and I was waiting to hear back on the furnishings quote." She couldn't understand what he was so worked up about. His eyes glittered dangerously at her, like she'd committed a cardinal sin.

"You don't clean, or do laundry, or...or..."

"Or what?"

"You just don't."

His mouth clamped shut. For a moment she was reminded of Matteo and his mutinous expressions when he didn't get his own way.

"Why not? Why shouldn't I do something useful?"

"Because that's not who you are. You are Anna Morelli."

She gaped. Her heart sank. Is that what he truly thought? "And that means what exactly? That I'm incapable of contributing? I'm not useful? What does that make me, Jace?

Decoration?"

Her throat tightened. "I spent many years with someone who thought just that. And I'll be damned if I'll do it again."

She started to stomp past him. After all she'd told him about Stefano, after all she'd revealed since her arrival. This is what it came to. He still saw the lines drawn between her world and his world. It had been the ruin of them before. He had learned nothing. These last days had only been a temporary respite.

"Anna, wait."

"No, I will not." She stomped her way to the stairs, halting for a moment with her hand on the newel post. "I tried to do you a favor by cleaning up after us all, but instead you've done me one. I fooled myself into thinking we'd both changed. But you're still as hung up on yourself as you ever were, and now I know how you really see me. You might be surprised at some of the things I've done."

His mouth took on an acidic twist. "I don't think you could surprise me at all."

She considered his words for a moment, knowing there was a hidden meaning, but there was too much going on now to bring something else into it. The truth was he'd always been so concerned with building himself and becoming a success that he'd missed things. Things that she hadn't.

"Where do you think I learned to keep house?"

"Does it matter?"

"Yes, I think it does. I was not self-reliant because that wasn't my position. But I knew how. Your mother taught me."

"Mom?"

"Yes, Mom. Did you know how hard it was for her to keep up when her arthritis flared? And you were off making your way in the world and ignoring what was before your eyes. She needed help, and in your absence I did it. In return I learned how to clean and launder and cook a little."

"You had your own household help but dusted my mother's furniture? I don't believe it."

"Someone had to."

For a moment she saw a flash of vulnerability in his eyes. Then it was gone. "I didn't know. But working hard was worth it."

He straightened his shoulders, emphasizing the broad expanse of his chest, and lifted his chin in defiance.

"Worth it," she repeated blankly.

"Mom doesn't have to clean or cook anymore. I've looked after her and Dad."

Anna shook her head. He honestly thought that throwing money at them was looking after them. He still didn't get it. He never had. Perhaps things had turned out the right way after all. Even though it hurt to admit it.

"I'll pack up the children and get out of your hair. Thank you for your *fine* hospitality," she added frostily.

"Stop."

The command echoed through the foyer as he stepped forward and grasped her wrist.

"Let go of me."

"Not yet."

"Jace." She turned her wrist but he held it fast.

"Not until you listen to me. I did not mean you were not useful. Of course not. But we are friends. You don't have to be useful."

"Yes, I do. And a real friend would understand that."

"Do you really have such a low opinion of yourself?"

She flushed. "That's not fair."

"You are better than a cleaning lady. You deserve more. You deserve…"

She took one step down so only one stair was between them.

"I know what I deserve," she answered in a low voice. "Do not put me on a Morelli pedestal anymore. I do not want to be there. There is no shame in doing honest work with your hands. At least I feel like I am being productive. Like I am contributing."

"You don't need to contribute. It is not what you were born for."

A hard ball of futility settled in her stomach. Not contribute? If she had nothing to contribute, whatever was she on this earth for, then? Did he really consider her above menial tasks? Or was there something more to it?

"Jace Willow, you are the worst kind of snob." She took the final stair down and twisted her wrist, setting it free. "You always were. You carry a chip on your shoulder about being poor. About wanting more. About what constitutes shame and embarrassment. My shame is not that I cleaned a house or changed a diaper. My shame is being so spineless that I settled for less than I should have all along."

"On that we agree, at least."

Her nostrils flared. "Yet you would do the same to me."

"I do not want to see you lowered."

"I have been as low as I ever care to go. I have not lowered myself. I have *freed* myself. There is a huge difference."

She spun away then and went upstairs.

Jace watched her go, confused. What the hell had just

happened? She was insulted? He'd been trying to say it wasn't necessary for her to be his cleaning lady. She was so much more. Didn't she realize how much? And she'd thrown it in his face and somehow made it his fault.

She deserved better. And yet she kept choosing the wrong way. Did she think this was a way to do penance for bad choices? Because she didn't belong in rubber gloves and an apron. She belonged in a beautiful dress with a glass of champagne in her hand. It was how he'd always seen her. She'd always been perfect to him. And he couldn't accept anything less, not now.

Because if she tumbled off of that pedestal, it was his fault, and he didn't think he could handle going through the guilt one more time.

He could see Matteo out of the window, kicking a ball on the grass, retrieving it and kicking it again. It looked lonely. It reminded him of himself as an only child, in the days before he'd had Alex to play with and Anna to torment.

He didn't want her to go. And it surprised him to realize he didn't want the children to go either. Despite never wanting any, he was starting to get used to their presence. Matteo had been a delight today at the boat dealer, full of childish enthusiasm but with good manners. Half of the excitement had been seeing the brown eyes widen with awe at the sleek powerboats.

He had to show Anna what he'd meant about the menial jobs. It angered him to think she now considered herself unworthy of fine things. She did deserve them. And more.

He opened the door and called out softly. "Matteo."

The brown-topped head tipped up and the ball bounced away.

"You want to help me with a surprise?"

"Mama, put on a dress."

Anna fastened the last tab on Aurelia's diaper and looked down at Matteo's face with indulgence. "A dress. Whatever for?"

"Please, Mama." He went to the closet and opened it, tugging on a linen sundress. "This is pretty. You put it on."

"What are you up to?"

She took the hanger with the dress out of the closet before he pulled it off. His eyes sparkled up at her and she couldn't help the smile that stretched across her face at his clear anticipation.

"You'll put it on, right?" He nearly bounced with anticipation.

She had an uneasy feeling in her stomach. "Won't you tell me why, Matteo?"

"It's a surprise. A secret. Please, Mama."

She couldn't say no to a face like that. "Oh, all right," she conceded, tipping his nose with a finger.

"I have to go. Put on the dress and come downstairs, okay?"

He ran back out of the room and she considered the dress.

What would it hurt? There had been harsh words between her and Jace this afternoon. Truthful words, but harsh nonetheless. She didn't want to fight with him. She'd never wanted to argue, not with Jace. With him, she'd always wanted…

She sighed, laying the dress across the bed. Who was she kidding? She'd always just wanted *him.* She'd adored him and for a short time he'd let her. He'd put down the wall between them and the summer had been magical. No pretense.

But then the world had changed and she'd become Anna Morelli again and he'd reverted to being the poor boy from down the hill. She had never cared about his status. He'd just been too stubborn to see it.

Once upon a time he'd looked at her, not with the derision of this afternoon, but with eyes bright with hunger at her mere appearance. For a brief time she'd felt cherished and loved. Desirable. When he came into the room he seemed to suck all the oxygen out, leaving her breathless and dazzled. When was the last time she'd truly felt that way? She trailed her fingers over the soft linen. Could she get him to look at her that way again?

Did she want him to? She'd vowed never to love again. But this wasn't love. This was...well, she didn't know what it was. Perhaps a way to find an end to something that had never really been finished.

Aurelia sat on the floor, attempting to stack blocks that kept toppling over. Anna changed, putting on the simple dress and then running her hands over the skirt. The fabric was cool and the pattern feminine. The tiny cap sleeves started off the shoulder. She looked in the mirror, grabbing at her hair and experimenting.

Her reflection sobered as it stared back at her. Her fingers held up the mass of hair, and she remembered how Jace had liked her hair up—and then enjoyed removing her pins one by one. The memory sent a skittering of pleasure over her skin.

She'd felt beautiful then, and suddenly she wanted to again. Perhaps this was a way of smoothing things over. And this time the children would be there to run interference. But she left the pins out of her hair. One didn't dare tempt fate too much.

With Aurelia on her arm, she went downstairs, her slippers

nearly silent on the hardwood steps. The front door was open, and as she went to shut it Matteo came steaming around the corner of the house, puffing and clearly on a mission.

"Slow down!" She held the door open for him as he came up the steps.

"You're supposed to come now," he said, holding out his hand.

"Tay-o!"

Anna looked at Aurelia, wondering what on earth...only to see the baby with her arms stretched out towards her brother. "Matteo?"

Aurelia pushed harder against Anna's arms as they went down the verandah stairs. At the bottom, Matteo held out his hands to his sister. Anna put Aurelia in his pudgy arms and stood back for a moment. So much like herself and Alex. She'd worshipped her brother and he'd been so good to her. Perhaps she was doing one thing right as a parent—it was clear they loved each other. "Why don't you hold her hands," she suggested to Matteo. He put Aurelia on the ground, took her hands in his, and helped her toddle off towards the river.

"Where are you going?"

"You need to come," was all Matteo would answer. She followed just behind them, enjoying the soft scent of the early evening. The sun was a warm ball in the sky, with the earlier hard edge of summer heat now dissipated. A perfect summer evening. Almost like she could remember from home, sitting on the velvety grass of the hill above the valley. Jace had chosen well.

She saw him waiting for her, and her heart stopped for one sweet second.

He stood by the willow, a large basket on a corner of a huge blanket. A picnic. Jace and Matteo had engineered a summer picnic.

Matteo and Aurelia tottered forward, but she paused. Even after the hurtful things he'd said today, he somehow still managed to have a grip on her heart. He couldn't know of course. Her life wasn't his, not anymore. His was business and being accountable to no one but himself. And hers was being accountable all the time to two most precious treasures. He didn't want children and she already had two. But that didn't stop the yearning, or the wanting, or the pulse of heat that throbbed through her each time their eyes met—like they were right now.

He'd changed into dark casual trousers and a fine summer shirt in beige, a color that should have been dull but that came to life against his tanned skin and dark hair. His hands were in his pockets, and it had been many years since she'd felt the urge to walk up to a man and kiss him just because she could. She wished she could do so now, but she wouldn't. Too much time had passed between them. They didn't have a future and to indulge in fantasy wouldn't help either of them. She was done with fantasies and fancies. It was just a shame that this particular setting was now the most romantic moment she'd experienced in a very long time.

"Come on, Mama!"

She made her feet move again.

"What have you done?" she asked as she reached the perimeter of the blanket.

"I made a picnic for dinner," he replied, gesturing for her to take a seat on the blanket. "Actually, we made the picnic, didn't we, Matteo?"

The boy nodded enthusiastically. "I helped."

"Of course you did. You're always helpful, sweetheart."

She slipped off her shoes and sat on the blanket, arranging

her skirt over her calves so only her toes peeked out.

"Mama, may I have a cracker?"

"Don't ask me, ask Jace. You two are the ones who packed the basket."

Jace grinned and she warmed. Perhaps some of those words had needed to be said this afternoon, to clear the air. The animosity of earlier had fled. Instead of feeling dictated to, she was feeling pampered.

Jace first handed her a glass of chilled Viognier. She took it from his hand, their fingers brushing. She couldn't meet his eyes. If she did she knew he'd see how a simple touch affected her.

"Matteo, you're in charge of helping your sister." Jace issued the instruction while Anna stared in surprise. He handed them a plate with crackers, tiny pieces of cheese, and baby-sized pieces of *proscuitto*. He fixed a similar plate for Anna, only in adult proportions, and then one for himself.

It was simple. It was perfect.

A flurry behind them announced a family of loons taking off from the river. Matteo pointed at them with a finger and Aurelia's mouth made an "O" in response. Jace looked at Anna and smiled.

And damn near broke her heart.

She hastily sipped some wine, trying to cover the expression she knew was on her face. He couldn't realize this was all she'd ever wanted. A simple picnic beneath a tree with her children and their father. Only he wasn't their father. He'd made that choice. And for him to make such a gesture now was bittersweet.

"Is everything all right?"

His voice sounded quietly concerned. She looked at the

children, laughing and eating together.

"I'm fine."

"Are you sure?"

Of course she wasn't sure, or fine, or any of those things. In a matter of less than a week, she was falling back in love with him. It had happened even knowing little had changed. They still had different priorities. What a fool she was.

She pasted on a bright smile. "Of course I'm sure."

"I wanted to apologize for this afternoon, you see. I think you misunderstood what I meant. The last thing I wanted to do is insult you. And I keep feeling like you're trying to punish yourself for something. My words about cleaning were..."

He stopped, swallowed. "I watched my mother work herself to the bone, watched my dad struggle to provide for us and I do not wish that for you. I want good things for you, Anna. You deserve them."

"I enjoy doing for myself now. Doing everyday tasks gives me a feeling of accomplishment. I enjoy it."

"I just don't want you to feel like you need to. I can afford to have a cleaning lady, I promise."

She leaned over and placed a hand on his arm, determined to tell him another truth even if it wasn't the wisest action.

"Jace...I couldn't care less if you can afford it or not. Those things don't matter to me."

His eyes cooled. "They matter to me."

She withdrew her hand. "I know they do. They always have." She couldn't keep the sadness out of her voice.

"I was only trying to be good enough for you."

Finally, some unvarnished truth. For some reason it was easier speaking this way than it had been before. "Money and things do not make you good enough for me. Stefano had those things but he was a failure as a husband and a father. Why are you so determined to make *things* matter?"

She already partially knew the answer. Because every moment of every day her father had hammered that message home. Jace wasn't good enough because he was poor. The irony was that Roberto had come from nothing, the second son of an Italian immigrant. When it came to his children, a different set of rules applied.

"Because a man provides for the woman he loves."

The moment halted. Instantly, Anna was transported back to when she had been barely out of adolescence, and Jace had been an energetic youth, full of dreams and plans. She had tried to convince him then that she didn't care if he could provide her with a house and servants and fancy dresses. But he hadn't listened. He'd been so determined to not let anything get in the way of his plans.

Back then he'd said the same thing. A man provides for the woman he loves. It had been his excuse for putting things off, and then for walking away. He hadn't been ready.

He was certainly well-off enough now, and here they were, still on opposite sides. She'd been right. There was too much history between them for them to ever go back. He still couldn't see material possessions were not what a woman needed most. Things couldn't feed the heart.

"And that's where we differ. A man loves a woman, and the rest works itself out. Look at your mama and papa."

He sat back, putting his plate aside and brushing his hands of crumbs. The children had abandoned their plates and were along the border of trees, picking dandelions and daisies. "My mama and papa were poor and tired. They struggled to put food on the table. They went without more than they should have, and all my father got for his trouble was a paycheck that was enough to get by and a bad back."

"Yes, that's true. But look at my father. He had everything...a profitable business. A lovely home, servants, luxury cars. And he was miserable. He'd had all those riches, but the woman he loved hadn't cared. And she broke his heart into tiny pieces. So who had the better life, I ask you?"

She paused. Jace was looking out over the water, his jaw set.

"I had a charmed life, and it got blown to hell. I would have traded it all for..."

"For what?"

He turned back to her.

How could she tell him that this was what she'd always wanted? A quiet and simple family evening? She had a fortune in the bank, and Aurelia and Matteo would never want for anything. Except for times like these. They could not be bought.

"I envied you your childhood, did you know that?" she replied, unwilling to vocalize her true thoughts.

"I never understood why."

"Because there was love and happiness. Because there were no expectations. You were allowed to be exactly who you were. It was a revelation to Alex and me. And yet, you were never satisfied."

"I was the poor kid."

"It didn't matter to me."

"It mattered to *me*, Anna. I always felt a few steps behind, like I had to catch up."

She held out her glass. "May I have more wine?"

He tipped the bottle, pouring more of the clear liquid into her glass.

"Does it feel odd, talking about all of this now? After so many years have passed?" She angled her head.

"Once upon a time, I would have quieted your chatter with a kiss." His voice was warm and melted over her nerve endings.

"Once upon a time, I would have pulled the pins from your hair."

Her pulse jumped as heat flooded her core. So much for time passing and moving on. All it took were softly spoken words on a blanket and she was as much his as she ever had been. "I...I didn't wear my hair up," she stammered, suddenly nervous.

"Once upon a time, Anna, I would have lain you on this blanket and made love to you in the sunset."

"Jace..."

His name was choked from her throat, the sound creating a delicious torture of memories. She wished he would lean forward, just a few inches. To feel his fingertips on her skin. To sneak a kiss while the children frolicked nearby. But instead he drained his wineglass and stared off at the children.

"But not now, right?" The words were so cold they felt like a slap. "You made the choice to give that all away the day you pledged to marry Stefano."

Chapter Seven

"That's not fair."

Jace looked away. He wasn't sure why he'd said it. A momentary impulse of truth perhaps? The fact that his shock had been utterly and completely real when the announcement of her marriage had been made? Maybe now she needed to realize just how much it had affected him.

But in this moment, it was a way to put distance between them because the memories were coming back and he didn't want to need her again. What he'd said before had been true too. He had been thinking of kissing her. Of touching her and making love to her. Not now, of course. But the memory of doing so in the past touched him so profoundly that it sparked a need in him. A need for her, and that would be a mistake.

He'd nearly given in to his need before, and all it had done was prove his point. He'd wanted to be wrong. He'd wanted to believe that Anna was different, from her father and the other spoiled girls that hung around Morelli. But in the end she hadn't been. And the truth of that still stung. No matter how much their friendship still meant, the fact remained that she'd gone ahead and married a man who could give her everything Jace couldn't.

He'd asked for time, and she hadn't waited. Of all the people in the world, he'd trusted her. He hadn't thought she was like the rest of the rich kids. And even though he knew he was partly to blame, her marriage to Stefano had still tasted like betrayal.

"Many things aren't fair. That's life, isn't it?"

He couldn't stop the hard edge to his voice any more than he could stop the memory of finding her with a ring on her finger when he'd returned from Kelowna. A ring that wasn't his, a two-carat stunner that glittered on her finger. Eighteen years old and a hurried engagement to another man to cover up their mistake—no, his mistake. It had been a punch to the gut, and he'd felt it each time since. Each time he'd seen her with her babies. Even the moment she'd arrived here, so obviously shattered, with that ring still on her hand. He looked down at her hands now. No gold or diamonds adorned the long fingers. She was no longer Stefano's. But neither was she his.

"I know you're angry with me..."

He sighed and began picking up the mess on the blanket. "I'm angry with a lot of things. Angry at your father for his narrow-minded views. I knew his ambition for you was always a good marriage. And yes, at you too. I was angry that you married Stefano, you're right. And I'm more angry that you turned your back on me."

"Why do you think I came to you?" The words were gentle, and she cocked her head slightly, as if waiting for an answer. Only she didn't wait, she kept on. "Don't you think I know how my father pushed? That I should have stood up to him more? Did you consider that maybe I wanted more for myself? But I went ahead and married his choice and it was a mistake. It cost me my friendship with you too. I have to live with that."

She lowered her gaze, a flush blooming on her cheeks. "I missed you, is that what you want to hear? And when my world came crashing down it was you I wanted to be with. It was you I thought would understand the most." She folded her hands. "And yet sometimes I feel like you understand nothing."

Jace put down the basket and looked at her. She was calm. Really calm, like she accepted everything. How could she, when he was struggling with it so much? How would she feel if she knew that as angry as he was, there was a small glimmer of something in him that made him happy she was free of Stefano?

And for what? He cared about her, it was true. His pulse quickened when she was around. But it was a giant leap from that to wanting everything. She wasn't the same girl she'd been then, and the grownup woman before him was even more alluring. It was becoming harder and harder to reconcile the two sides of her—the woman who'd thrown their chance at a family away, to the one who claimed family meant everything now.

The trouble was he wanted to believe in her. He'd gambled on a lot of things over the years, but he wasn't sure he had enough daring for this.

"Why don't we just leave it behind for tonight? I told Matteo we'd go tomorrow, but let's take the boat for a ride up the river." He wanted to see a smile on Matteo's face. Little things the boy said told Jace his childhood thus far hadn't been ideal. And he wanted to see the wind in Anna's hair. To see her smile, to be in the moment and not the past.

"He would love that."

"And you?"

She tried a smile, but it wobbled. "Me too."

Jace watched as she called the children over and then pointed to the boat bobbing gently next to the dock. He was glad he'd bought it. He was gladder still that he could buy it. He hadn't been able to do such things even a few years ago. But now...he'd built the business enough that he could afford such things. Perhaps this was not a boat like Stefano had had. But his sails would serve no purpose here on the river, and a sleek little motorboat was just the thing. Jace hadn't been in a position to provide things for her back then, but he could now and he wanted her to know it.

"Everyone ready?"

He got in first, lifted Matteo over the side and then reached for Aurelia. Anna paused and then placed the baby in his hands.

He realized it was the first time he'd held Aurelia since the bee-sting incident and she stared up at him with wide brown eyes. Unblinking, she watched him and then placed a small hand on his lower lip and pulled. Her weight felt foreign, but he couldn't say it was a bad thing. He wondered if perhaps this wasn't a good idea. She was so small, and suddenly he felt responsible for her welfare. Not because he had to be but...

"Ba, ba," she babbled and patted his mouth.

He couldn't help the smile that curved along his cheek. "Ba ba to you too," he replied, shifting her into one arm and holding out a hand to help Anna get in last.

She'd taken off her sandals and left them on the dock. Placing her hand in his, she stepped barefoot into the boat, and for a moment they both paused.

Her hand in his. Her baby on his arm.

And the uneasy feeling that there was a rightness to it.

"There are lifejackets for everyone," he said quietly, dropping her hand. He kept Aurelia on his hip, her weight surprisingly comfortable as Anna fastened hers around her waist and then helped Matteo buckle his. No one spoke. He wondered if she were thinking about Stefano, and how he had drowned. There had been no question when he'd bought the boat. Everyone would have life vests and wear them. Even little Aurelia, whose orange jacket crowded her chin and made her fuss.

Jace noticed the white line around Anna's lips and wondered if this was her first time on the water since Stefano's accident. He hadn't given it a thought. She was hiding her fear and he sought to reassure her.

"I won't go too fast, I promise."

"I trust you, Jace."

Her face was white and he reached down and cupped her jaw. "Thank you."

He wouldn't break that trust a second time. He vowed it as he turned the key and started the engine.

"She'll be fine once we're moving," he suggested, pulling on his own vest and zipping it up. The low rumble filled the air, making Matteo's eyes widen. Jace untied them from the dock and gently pushed away. He looked back. Anna was sitting with Aurelia on her lap and Matteo close beside her. A mother bear protecting her cubs. His heart clubbed at the sight of them. He would look after them. He wished she understood that.

At the touch of a button the motor lowered into the water, and Jace tested the throttle, propelling them forward.

"Mama!"

Anna turned her head. "Yes, sweeting?"

"We're moving."

Jace hid a smile. He knew exactly how Matteo was feeling. Now this was a toy that was fun. These were the kinds of things he'd missed growing up and had experienced vicariously through his association with the Morellis. He steered them around the bend in the river, and suddenly the sparkling water lay spread out before them. He looked back, grinned and pushed the throttle forward. Anna's eyes widened and he let off...not too fast.

The boat leapt over the water and Jace's hair blew off his face. The wind was cool and soft from the water. They were alone on the river tonight. He looked back to see Matteo with wide eyes taking in everything on the riverbanks and Anna, holding Aurelia in her arms. Aurelia had quieted and her mouth made a tiny, perfect "O" as she pointed a chubby finger at a crane that took off, wide wings flapping and legs dangling, as the boat disturbed the peace. Anna's smile was soft and warm, and her hair blew back from her neck in long, rich waves.

He swallowed thickly and turned back to face the front, steering down the middle of the river with the sun flickering through the trees. This family could have been his. But did he want it? He had a good life. He was free to do what he wanted, when he wanted. By relying on his own judgment and wits, he'd bought Two Willows and made it flourish, and now he was expanding. He could provide for his parents. He knew better than most that nothing came without sacrifice. Being lonely now and again had been a small price to pay. And he was smart enough to know that the impulses he was feeling where Anna was concerned had more to do with what had happened in the past than with what he really wanted in the present.

Which was stupid. Because the past was done and couldn't be changed.

He would be Uncle Jace, not Papa, and that was just fine.

After several minutes he turned in a half circle and slowed, leaving the boat to idle gently as it bobbed on the waves of their wake.

"That was fun." Matteo's eyes danced. He stood from his seat, staggering a little at the uneven footing. Jace shot out a hand and gripped his arm, flashing a smile at the alarm that had flickered in the boy's eyes.

"Would you like to drive?"

"Me?"

"Are you sure it's all right, Jace?" Anna interrupted and he turned to see a furrowed brow above worried eyes.

"He will be safe," Jace assured her. "I promise."

"Sit here, on my knee." He patted his leg and Matteo climbed aboard. "I'll make us go a little faster, like this." He put his hand on the throttle, moving them forward slowly. "You put your hands on the wheel here, and you steer."

Matteo's hands gripped the wheel, his arms stiff.

"Relax. I'll make us go a little faster, okay? And you will turn us in a circle."

He sped up slightly, then guided Matteo's hands as they went around. They were nearly facing upriver again when Matteo turned his head and looked up at Jace, grinning from ear to ear. "I did it."

Jace's heart thudded. He looked so much like Alex. He wondered if Anna saw the resemblance to Matteo's true uncle. Or if she looked at him and saw Stefano.

"Do you want to take us home?"

He nodded. "Okay."

"Maybe next time we'll let your mama drive, hmmm?"

"Mama says she is scared of the water."

Matteo kept his hands on the wheel, but Jace went still. He looked back at her to see if she'd heard. Her face was pure white. Why would she be afraid? They had always gone swimming as children. Perhaps it was because of Stefano. He knew her well enough to know even as unhappy as she'd been, she never would have wanted Stefano to suffer such a fate. She wasn't that cruel. Perhaps his accident had left more of an

111

indelible mark than he'd originally thought.

"Forgive me, Anna. I didn't realize. I..." But he didn't know what else to say, not with Matteo sitting on his knee. The boy didn't need to hear them talk about how his father died.

Anna knew what Jace was thinking, but correcting him was impossible. "It's okay. They say you should do that which you are afraid of."

The words drifted away on the slight wind created by the boat, but stuck in Anna's chest. There were so many things she was afraid of, and she'd come here to hide away from them. Only to be faced with the biggest fear of all.

She was falling for Jace all over again.

He smiled at her and it hurt her deep inside. Never would she have imagined him being so good with her children. The way he'd been patient with Matteo, taking the time to show him...it was something that Stefano had never done.

She'd stepped onto the boat to prove something to both of them. To prove to Jace she was independent and that he didn't affect her. To prove to herself she could do it. To face the demon and make it go away. All of it had backfired. He hadn't been reckless or any of the things she kept telling herself he was. He'd been caring and respectful and generous.

He'd become the boy he'd been back then. The one she'd loved unreservedly. Knowing those qualities were still inside him, she was deathly afraid that if she weren't careful, he'd have the means to break her heart all over again.

They went back to Two Willows at a much slower pace, Matteo loving every second at the wheel. Jace pointed out several osprey nests along the way, and once they saw one dive and rise up with a salmon in its talons. Matteo was suitably thrilled, and from the look on Jace's face, he was enjoying

112

himself too. These sorts of moments were something she hadn't considered until now. But Matteo was loving having a male presence in his life. Even these few moments were more than Stefano had ever bothered with.

That first night Jace had been so uptight, worrying about messes, and she'd felt the censorious glare on her back as she'd tended to the children. But in the last few days he had relaxed. He was good with them, and they responded to him. Today alone, he'd taken Matteo shopping for a boat, had concocted a picnic, and now their dark heads were pressed together as they steered the boat home.

The idea put a small dent in her heart. But it wouldn't work. It wouldn't be fair to Matteo or Aurelia. They would only get attached and have to leave again. Her life was not here. She was only here to figure out what to do next. And what was best for her children was consistency.

And then the two of them laughed and Anna tried very hard not to make wishes. Sometimes, when she and Jace weren't arguing, it felt right.

When they got back, he tied up the boat and got out first, then took the children and Anna last. She refused to meet his eyes. She didn't want him to see her feelings, and right now they were riding very close to the surface.

"I didn't know you were afraid," he murmured as Matteo took enjoyment from tossing the lifejackets onto the seats of the boat. "I should have realized...after the accident."

He did think it was all about Stefano, then. Knowing it was something else entirely made physical pain cut into her like a knife, stinging and sharp. Now he was being solicitous and it was lovely. It was a gesture of peace. And damned if it didn't endear him to her all the more. He couldn't know that his kindness hurt her almost as much as his harsh words of the afternoon had.

"My fear of the water isn't rational, and I didn't want to deny the children—or you—the enjoyment. I had to do it sometime."

"I had hoped you would have fun too. That perhaps there hasn't been much fun lately." He squeezed her fingers. "Anna," he prodded.

She looked up at him, then turned a half-turn and walked to the end of the dock, back to firm land again. It felt good and reassuring under her feet. Despite their arguments, somehow today a bridge had been built between them, and she trusted him enough to give him a glimpse of what had really transpired in her disaster of a marriage.

"We fought about the sailboat," she admitted quietly. "I did not want him to buy it. But he did anyway, and then took great pleasure in disappearing on it. It was his way of getting away from me, from our marriage. And he never let me forget it."

"I'm sorry."

"No, I am sorry. I made the decision to marry him and I did it for the wrong reasons. There is no excuse for it. And yet..." She looked ahead and saw Matteo and Aurelia picking daisies. Three blossoms were clutched firmly in Matteo's chubby hand. "I didn't think it was possible to love anyone as much as I love my children."

He stopped her with a hand on her arm. Why was he looking at her with awe and yet a flicker of pain tightening his face? Surely he didn't share the same regrets. Yet somehow in this particular moment something moved between them.

"You are a good mother, Anna."

At this moment there was no other compliment he could have paid that would have meant as much.

"You are very good with them," she conceded. "I'm not sure who is more surprised—me or you."

And again a flicker of hurt, where she'd intended none. His dark eyes plumbed hers. "They are beautiful like their mother. I have no choice."

"Oh, Jace," she sighed. How she wished she could turn back the clock. "Sometimes I wish…" Her voice trailed off as she held back, not knowing how to put her longings into words.

"What do you wish?"

There was an edge to his voice and all she wanted to say remained boxed up inside. Now she understood why they'd avoided each other so much. Because being together reminded her of what it was like to love him. To confide in him. He'd been there for her ever since her mother had gone away. But that closeness was what kept them apart now. It nearly overwhelmed her.

It was perhaps better if they kept a respectful distance. Just enough to maintain the friendship, nothing more.

Being close reminded her of what it was to be loved by him, in all ways. But there was too much holding them apart now. Her job was with Morelli. Her father hated him as much as he ever did. Jace wasn't about to give up Two Willows and there was the much larger matter of their feelings, past and present. She knew she couldn't survive trying again and failing. The first time had nearly destroyed her.

Before she could reconsider, she stood on tiptoe and pressed a kiss to his cheek.

"Thank you for the evening. I did enjoy it. Truly. But I should get the children to bed."

"Of course, the children. They do keep you out of some sticky conversations, don't they?" He frowned a little, knowing his voice was hard with disappointment and unable to change it. This was becoming a pattern of hers, he realized. Hiding behind the children when things got too close. He dropped her hand and stepped back. Just when he thought she was going to give him a little honesty, she backed away.

"Jace—"

"You keep hiding and I don't know why. You are changed. You are not the Anna I remember, though I'm still not sure if I ever knew who that was. There are so many things that don't add up. And the moment we get close, you run away. I truly did not know you were afraid of the water. And I do not understand why I had to hear it from a four-year-old first."

There was a sinking feeling in his chest that all their progress was for nothing, but things needed to be said. "You would never have told me about the fights about the boat if Matteo hadn't spoken up."

"Probably not."

"Why?"

She looked down. "Because it is hard revealing all my mistakes."

"Your mistakes? Surely you don't blame yourself for everything." Jace should know. He'd played a big enough part. He never should have left her alone.

"Maybe I don't want you to know what a weak woman I've become."

Words sat on the edge of his tongue but he paused. No, enough. "This is me you're talking to."

She lifted her chin and her dark eyes glittered at him. "I know. That's the problem."

And to think he'd been on the verge of wanting to love her again. Now he was the problem. Anger flared up and lashed out.

"I do not understand why you came to me and then treat

me like the enemy."

"You are not the enemy," she whispered.

"It feels like it," he responded and strode away, leaving her standing on the dock with the children frolicking close by, unaware.

Chapter Eight

Anna tucked the blanket firmly around Matteo and felt her eyes fill with tears as she looked down on his sleeping form. He looked so small, so innocent with his lashes lying against his cheeks. She had made many mistakes, but it was very hard to regret them when her son and daughter were the results.

Jace had been right and it pained her to even admit it to herself. She didn't want to argue anymore. She didn't want to be old friends one moment and then fighting about things that were steeped in resentments from the past. It wasn't good for them, and it wasn't good for the children either. And so, as she pressed a kiss to Matteo's warm cheek, she knew she had to have the conversation she'd been putting off for over ten years.

They had to talk about the baby they'd never had.

Her stomach was a mass of knots thinking about it, yet in her heart she was sure it was the right thing. They had never spoken of it and it stood like a concrete wall between them even though they pretended otherwise. Quietly, she descended the stairs to look for him. She found him on the back deck of the house, a glass of dark liquor in his hands.

Anna shut the door behind her quietly but knew he was aware of her presence by the way his fingers tightened on the glass and his shoulders stiffened. She would have to be very careful. She wanted this conversation to solve things, not make them worse. And yet everything about his stance told her he was gearing for confrontation.

"The children are asleep?"

"Yes."

"Brandy?"

"No, thank you."

He kept his back to her and she inhaled, gathering strength, searching for the right words. A soft breeze shushed through the leaves of the trees in the twilight, and down at the river the peepers chirped, a sweet, syncopated rhythm. And then she heard him sigh.

That one sound touched her heart in ways she hadn't expected. She was kidding herself in calling Jace her friend. He had always been so much more, and she now realized that her coming here had not only been difficult for her, but for him as well. She knew what her regrets were. Did he have any? More than ever she wanted to bridge the gap between them.

"You are right in that I've been avoiding opening up to you."

He kept his back to her, but his voice was clear, strong. "Why? I thought we were supposed to be friends. You told me you wanted to come here, that you felt safe."

"In some ways I do. And in other ways..." She spoke into the darkness, letting it provide a little bit of protection. Secrets seemed softer out of the garish light of day. And yet this one seemed to cling to the years of silence. The one thing she'd never discussed with anyone. Not Alex, not Stefano, not even Mama Willow. "In other ways you are so dangerous, Jace."

She knew he understood when he didn't challenge her response. In his silence, she heard acceptance, but more than that. She heard agreement, and it sent desire crashing through her veins. Perhaps it was no more over for him either. And they were both playing with fire.

"I avoided speaking of it because I don't want to ruin what friendship remains between us," she explained.

"There was more than friendship once."

"I know. Once, I loved you."

She saw his fingers close tighter around his glass, saw his shoulders grow taut with tension.

The words slid out, but by putting them deliberately in the past tense it felt like something was over. There was a sense of loss and a tiny bit of grief as she recognized it.

"I loved you too, Anna."

"You say that now, but—"

"But I tried to say it then too. And I don't think you ever really believed in me. Perhaps if you had, you would have waited."

And even now he wouldn't look at her. But there was no mistaking the pain and resentment in the words. He was so still. Like he was bracing himself for something. Only she was no threat. Why couldn't he understand that?

He lifted his glass, took a drink, still staring out over the lawn.

"You hate me for marrying Stefano, don't you?"

"I could never hate you," he answered quietly.

"Oh, but I think you could. You can. You do."

She folded her hands, wanting to go to him but knowing it was better if she did not. If she went to him, she might never get the truth. And as difficult as it was, she knew only the truth would do tonight. If she went to him she would touch him, and she might never say what needed to be said.

"Anna."

"Why do you hate me, Jace? Just say it. Be free of it." She goaded him, wishing he'd do something, wishing he'd just be honest and get it out so they could deal with it. She needed him. And he wasn't hers in any way until he let go of whatever was keeping that wall erected between them.

He turned and faced her, leaned his back against the railing. His face remained closed off as he swirled the brandy in his glass, then took a sip. "What good would it do?" he remarked after he'd swallowed the liquor. "It's over and done."

"No, it's not." She took one hesitant step forward. "It's not done, not at all. No matter how much we want it to be. After what you said down by the river…"

"I'm sorry." He looked away and took another drink. Like that would fix everything.

She tapped her foot. God, she hadn't thought she'd have to drag everything out of him. She was tired of the hurtful comments that came out of nowhere, of the bickering that spoke of so much beneath the surface. But perhaps fighting was the one way to get him to say what he really meant.

"That's not good enough, not now. I'm tired of sorry. I'm tired of hearing it and I'm tired of saying it, and I want us to talk about it so we can move on."

His chin lifted a little as he snorted. "Yes, you're a great one for moving on."

"You see? That's the kind of thing I mean. We try to preserve what there is of our friendship, but then you make hurtful comments like that and we're back to where we started. Only each time it chips away a little more at the…" She paused on the word. What was between them? She couldn't bring herself to say the word love in reference to the present. "The regard we have for each other. Just say it. Just say that you blame me."

"I blame you. Satisfied?" His chin jutted out mutinously and she was once again reminded of Matteo. Which was silly, since Matteo was Stefano's child. But the expression was yet another hurtful reminder of what could have been.

"I'm hardly satisfied with that answer." She stared at him as he turned away again, shutting her out. And her own anger bubbled up inside. He blamed her, but he had played his own part too. He had to know that.

"Then what do you want from me, Anna?"

The question echoed around them, through the backyard and was lost in the flutter of the leaves.

"I want you to forgive me." She took a step forward. "I need to forgive you. But you know, first I think we really need to decide what for. We've never talked about what happened after you left for Kelowna with Alex. What do you blame me for, Jace? For moving on when you left me? You said you were not ready for anything permanent. You said you had too many things to do before you could consider settling down with someone and starting a family. You said we were too young. And then you left. Was I not free to be with someone else?"

Her mouth snapped shut. She hadn't meant to throw Stefano in his face. But remembering how abandoned she'd felt, the barb had come out anyway. He'd known how her mother's abandonment had hurt her, and yet he'd done the same thing. She couldn't back away now. She stepped closer so that his profile was in view.

His jaw ticked as he clenched his teeth. "Theoretically."

She huffed.

He held the glass so tightly she could see the half-moons of his fingernails. Getting anything out of Jace was like getting water from a stone. Perhaps it wasn't worth it. Perhaps too much had happened and she should just leave now. She tossed her hair over her shoulder and spun away.

Until his hoarse voice stopped her in the dark.

"Two months. Two months and I return to find you at your engagement party. Technically you were free, but your change of heart was certainly..."

She turned back at the pause. Her mouth dropped open as one cruel eyebrow lifted, challenging. He drained the glass and put it down on the railing. "Enlightening."

He had no idea then. He thought she'd married Stefano because she hadn't cared for him. Nothing could have been further from the truth. Had he really expected to leave and then come back to find her waiting? Had he thought her feelings had been false?

Had she hurt him?

"You didn't want me, Jace. You made that clear. You said you didn't want a wife and a...a..."

She couldn't say it. The word just wouldn't come, but they both knew what it was.

"I didn't know what I wanted. I was young. We both were." He pushed a hand through his hair. "God, we were so young. I was afraid. I needed time to think, and so I went with Alex to Kelowna. I never expected to come back to you engaged to someone else."

He did sound hurt. Like somehow all that had happened had been her fault. She'd been little more than a child. She hadn't known what to do. She'd only known that the man she loved didn't love her back, not the way he'd promised.

"You never said you needed time to think. To my recollection, you were very clear on what you didn't want. You didn't want me, and you didn't want the baby I was carrying."

There, she'd said it. She made herself hold his gaze. "If I

hadn't been engaged, would it have made a difference?"

"Yes."

Her heart trembled. His answer was so definitive, and the meaning of it rippled through her. She remembered seeing him for the first time when he'd returned. He'd been so cold to her, and she'd countered by being flippant and pert. She had been as low as it was possible to go, and it had taken every last bit of pride to face him. It had been the only way she could think of to keep from revealing her heartbreak in front of him. She'd thought him completely indifferent.

Hadn't he been?

"Easily said now." She didn't want him to make her doubt her decisions. She'd been doing that enough herself. And his words did nothing to placate her. She'd never taken him for a coward, but this certainly felt like he was taking the easy way out.

He pushed away from the rail, knocking the glass off into the grass below. In two strides he was before her, and his fingers gripped her upper arms, the tips digging into the flesh there. "Don't. Don't do that. Not once have I ever said something to you that I didn't mean. You swore to me that summer that you loved me. And weeks after we broke things off, you'd given your heart, your body..." his voice shivered, "...to another."

"Oh, I know you meant everything you said! You said you didn't want me or the baby. That was crystal clear. You said you loved me too. And then you left. So don't you dare question my actions."

"I left because I didn't know what to do. My God, Anna. I was trying to go to school, and work, and I was so full of you it was frightening. Then you were there telling me you were pregnant. I can't explain what I felt. Fear, certainly. And confusion. There was so much all at once and I needed quiet to think. Couldn't you have waited?"

His hands were hurting her arms, but she lifted her chin and looked at him, her eyes and nose stinging as she spoke the absolute truth in her heart. "I would have waited, if you'd asked me to."

He dropped her arms and stepped back.

"Did you hate me so much," he said, his voice barely more than a hoarse whisper.

"I didn't hate you, Jace. I loved you as much as it was possible for a girl to love a boy."

The dim light from the kitchen glowed through the window, so that the shadows on his face suddenly looked weary. "Then why, Anna?"

"I wanted everything from you and you pushed me away. Your face when I told you about the baby...you said you didn't want a wife and children and you said you needed to get away. Away from me. The next thing I knew you were gone and I was at the villa all alone.

"Then Stefano was there. He was what everyone seemed to think I should have. He came from a good family and he had money. My father loved him and kept saying how I'd be secure with him. So I did the 'right' thing. And I was so hurt that a part of me wanted to show you that I was wanted. You kept claiming we had to wait, that the time wasn't right because you hadn't accomplished what you wanted. And I said I didn't care about those things. But you did, Jace. You cared about them more than about me. You had to have, because you left to find them and left me alone, and scared, and pregnant. I married Stefano, because to me, I'd already lost the life I wanted."

His face hardened. His cheekbones were chiseled slabs and his eyes glittered darkly in the dim light. "Don't."

"Don't what? Don't talk about it? We have to. It's standing between us and always will."

"Anna!"

The command was dark with warning. Anna couldn't understand why he was so angry. His fingers balled into each other, flexing and unflexing next to his thighs, and she could sense the tension vibrating off him like a tuning string. He hadn't wanted the baby. He'd said so.

"Admit it, Jace," she continued. She had to. It had been a cloud over them all these years, and she knew their past was why he'd stayed away as much as he had. All the rest...the friendship, the so-called loyalty, it had all been for show when this truth had been simmering below the surface. Now it was time for the volcano of it to blow and be done with.

"Admit it. Admit you didn't want the baby or me. Admit that you came back and you were relieved."

"That's what you think?"

There was power, real force behind the words, and for a moment she got the feeling he was going to come over and shake her. But instead he twisted and strode off the deck into the darkness, his shoes making soft sounds on the grass as he walked away.

Had she been wrong?

She lifted trembling fingers to her lips. Had she miscalculated, then? The pain of that September came rushing back. Of losing Jace, and then losing the one thing of his she'd wanted most. Nothing had mattered. Stefano had appeared and she'd married him, as much to prove a point as to get out of the Morelli villa and the memories it held.

And the whole time she'd told herself that Jace had gotten exactly what he'd desired. His freedom.

Perhaps she'd been wrong. And so she went after him.

He stood next to a maple tree, his hand braced on the trunk so that she could see the outline of his broad shoulders in the moonlight. "Jace," she murmured, reaching out, then pulling her hand back.

"Go away, Anna."

"No, not this time."

His laugh was bitter. "Oh sure, now you choose to stay."

"It strikes me as ironic, that you accuse me of running when it was you who went away."

"I know. But isn't that what you did with Stefano? Use him to run away?"

"Yes."

He hadn't expected her to admit it, she was sure. Slowly, his hand came away from the tree and he faced her. He put his hands in his pockets and she faced him, determined to be truthful and quit hiding.

"You should know, Anna, I came back from Kelowna thinking I'd been a fool. I was going to do right by you. And do you know what I saw?"

"No," she whispered.

His eyes were unrelenting. Black and glittering, pinning her to the spot while the breeze ruffled her skirt around her calves.

"You look very much like you did that night. You were in a pale dress, and there was a breeze off the hills. I caught you on the terrace. The woman who was supposedly carrying my child. Only she was celebrating her engagement to another man. I wanted to ask you then and there, but we were interrupted. Then you were gone for a few weeks, shopping for your wedding, spending time with Stefano's family. I waited for you to come back. But when you did…"

He suddenly stopped talking. Anna looked up at him, unsure of where he was going with it all. "When I did..." she prompted, but he had broken eye contact at last. She saw him swallow, heard his ragged breathing.

"When I saw you again, I counted the weeks. And I realized you were as slim and beautiful as you had been in the summer when you'd told me about the baby. And that's when I knew. That's when I knew you had severed all ties with me completely. There was no baby. You'd made sure of it."

Anna's stomach dropped as the meaning of what he was saying slammed into her. That's what he thought? That she'd deceived him in that way? "Are you accusing me of lying about being pregnant? Of trying to trap you?" Disappointment was bitter in her mouth. "That cheapens what we had together."

"Oh, I believe you were pregnant. I saw your paleness in the mornings, the way you nibbled on bread and crackers from the kitchen at any time of day. But when I left, you made sure there was nothing for me to come back to. Nothing. And I hated you for it. Almost as much as I hated myself."

It registered then what he was saying, and grief struck her, fresh and sharp, stealing her breath. That time had been so difficult, but now, now she knew exactly what Jace had thought of her. Very little. It hurt more than she thought possible.

"You think I terminated the pregnancy?"

"What better way to exorcise yourself of anything tying you to me? I left you so you reacted and hit me back where it hurt. I couldn't believe you were capable of it, but the truth doesn't lie. When I came back you were not pregnant. When you married Stefano you were not pregnant. I know."

Tears quivered on her lashes. Tears of pain and anger and crushing disappointment that he could think she was capable of such a thing.

"You are wrong," she whispered, unable to keep from crying, the words coming out disjointed. "You stupid, stupid man. I did not have an abortion. *Dio mio.*" In her emotion she reverted back to the Italian that her father insisted be spoken at Morelli.

"Anna—"

She held up her hands. She did not want him to look at her, to touch her, to speak to her.

"No. I did not, and it kills me to think you thought I could have. No, Jace, I lost the baby, your baby, all alone, while you were out painting the town in Kelowna. While you were cruising the lake with Alex and having a great old time."

His gaze was dangerous in the darkness. "You are telling me you had a miscarriage?"

"Yes." The word came out on a gasp, almost as if the pain were as fresh as if it had been yesterday. Her fingers drifted down to her stomach. She'd wept the day it had happened, and every day for several months.

Even on her wedding day to another. And that in itself carried a little bit of guilt.

"I thought you—"

"You thought I did it to what? Get back at you? To pretend that it had never happened?" It crushed her to think he'd thought so little of her.

He swore and a soft smile formed on her lips at the choice of words, before fluttering away with the capriciousness of the breeze, leaving a gaping hole of sadness.

"It was my fault. I left you alone and I thought you had an...an...that you got rid of it because you were ashamed."

Before she could reconsider, she stepped forward and cupped his jaw in her hand, making him look at her. "*Never.*

Never ashamed. I would have had your baby anyway. I would have endured the whispers and the looks just to know that we created a miracle together. Loving you was beautiful. Making love with you was my choice. I wanted you. I wanted your love. I wanted your baby. But when I lost it..."

Anna closed her eyes for a moment. Even though she'd been heartbroken that he had left her, she'd cherished the life growing within her. It was a product of their love. With or without Jace, she would have borne his child without question. And would have been proud.

"When you lost the baby..."

There was something in his voice now. Something hesitant and soft, almost a plea for her to say the right thing. She didn't know what it was he needed, and so she knew she simply had to tell the truth so they could deal with it. She placed her other hand on his face, framing it with her fingers.

"When I lost the baby, and you were gone, and we were over...there was no point to anything anymore. I was alone. The last time I'd been so alone was when Mama left us all. All I wanted was that piece of you that would belong to me. And..."

She stopped again, dropping her eyes so he couldn't see the awful pain there. She couldn't get into the details of how it had happened. It hurt too much, still now. And what would it possibly solve? Nothing.

"And it was gone."

"Yes." She dropped her hands.

The air in his lungs came out in a whoosh. "All this time I thought you'd hated me so much that you...that you'd been so desperate to keep us a secret that..."

"Never," she whispered. "It breaks my heart to know you think I would do that. Not after all we shared that summer."

"I was going to come back and marry you, Anna."

Tears for the life she could have had came hot and burning. She blinked. "Dammit."

"And you were with him. And I blamed myself. I waited too long. I was a coward. I deserved that you moved on."

Even in the darkness she could sense the pain and self-loathing in his voice, and it broke her heart all over again. She wanted to reach out and touch him again, but there was so much pain it still kept a wall between them.

"We both made so many mistakes," she whispered. "Please believe me. I did not have an abortion. When I lost the baby, I felt there was nothing left for me. You were gone. What else could I think beyond you did not love me? I no longer had a reason for getting up in the morning. I felt myself withering away, and then there was Stefano."

She sighed. "I told myself I didn't care about anything so marrying Stefano meant nothing. But I was young, and a part of me wanted to show you. Wanted to show you that someone wanted me. Wanted to show you what you'd walked away from. And I wanted desperately to get out of that house. I couldn't stand to hear Father speak against you. Stefano was my ticket out, and nothing else mattered."

"It worked. I never got over feeling like Stefano had stolen my life. But what was worse was that I let it happen. I didn't fight for you. I'm not proud of myself."

"So you stayed away."

"It hurt too much to see you. You looked happy. You had the children and every time I saw them I was reminded of..."

The words went unspoken, but they both knew he had been reminded of their child who had never been born.

"I don't know what to say."

"You have to understand. I thought that you had chosen. You had chosen to bear his children but not mine. And in a way I hated you both for it."

He stopped.

"I am not a good man, Anna."

Her heart melted at his confession. It hurt that he'd thought she'd deliberately ended her pregnancy, but less now that she understood it was coming from a place of pain. Regret flooded her. If only they could have had this conversation then. Things would have been different.

"You *are* a good man. You always have been. We were just young, and we did it wrong."

It was new ground, common ground, acknowledging both their mistakes and somehow managing to forgive each other for them. For the first time in over a decade, Anna felt like their bond was strong enough to withstand anything. Like a piece that had been missing was back in place.

"How did it happen?"

She was silent for a long moment. This would be the hardest, because explaining it meant reliving it, and there had already been so much brought to the surface today.

"Please," he whispered, and again she caught the tight string of hurt beneath the words. "It was my baby too."

She swallowed, knowing he deserved the truth but unsure of how she could possibly tell it. "I don't know if I can do this," she murmured, trying hard to swallow the saliva pooled in her mouth. "I can't, Jace."

He reached out and held her hand. His fingers linked with hers and she took a deep breath. He did deserve to know. They had come this far. And so she squeezed his fingers in hers. Needing that link between them, strong and solid.

"I had gone to the stream," she said softly, closing her eyes. She couldn't look at him while she told it, but closing her eyes was almost worse. When she closed her eyes she was right back there again, like no time had passed at all.

"I went there a lot," she said, forcing herself to continue. "I would sit by the bank and remember what it had been like to be held in your arms. The glory of making love to you. You, my first lover. To me, you were perfect. And even though you had left me, somehow I clung to a bit of hope that one day you would come back and find me sitting there waiting for you on the grass, and you would tell me it was all a mistake."

"So close..." he whispered, the words carried away with the shush of the wind in the trees. But they both knew it. It might have been that way. If only...

"I had been feeling odd all morning. I wasn't sleeping well, but then I wanted to sleep all the time, and I wasn't eating right, just nibbling to try to keep away the nausea. I hadn't told anyone about the baby. I was keeping it to myself, knowing there was a little part of you growing inside me. I wanted to hold it close inside, our secret, something private and wonderful. I was afraid to tell my father. He was already so protective of me. If he'd known about you and I...and I wasn't ready to let it end.

"But then the cramping started. I thought maybe it was okay and that the cool water would soothe me, so I went into the stream. It was so refreshing, and I felt so light. But the cramps got worse. Sharper, like when I had a bad period, and I got scared. I came out of the water, wet...and there was blood running down my leg."

When she got to the end, her voice broke. "It was gone, Jace. Just like that. I kept saying over and over, 'don't take my baby', but no one heard me. And I tried to scrub away the blood and pretend it wasn't happening, but it was and then I just knew it was gone. This baby that neither of us had planned and that was going to cause a holy uproar, and suddenly I couldn't bear to lose it. You were gone. The baby was gone. I had nothing left. I was just...empty."

Her breath caught on a sob.

And then his arms were around her, holding her close, and she was crying into his shirt, smelling the scent that was Jace—man and clean laundry and safety. He had always smelled like that. She had needed him for so long and finally he was here. Only it was too late to change anything or make anything right, and for the first time since that day, she let herself truly grieve for what she'd lost. Him. Their life together. And their child.

"I should have been there." The words were husky and warm through her hair. "I let you down. I'm so sorry. I should have been there for you through it all."

"I wanted you so much, but I knew I couldn't call you. You said you didn't want the baby."

"That's what I thought. That's what I told myself because I was so scared. Oh, Anna, is that why you don't like the water anymore?"

She nodded. "Every time I feel it on my skin, I remember."

He took a ragged breath. "I am so sorry you went through that alone."

"I wasn't all alone. I went to your mother," she said, taking a shuddering breath and trying to regain some bit of composure. "I couldn't go home. I didn't know where else to go. She took one look at me and my clothes and knew exactly what had happened. She..." Anna stopped for a moment, trying to keep in control, barely managing. "She gave me a warm bath, and a glass of wine, and a shoulder. And then she took me to a doctor for an examination."

He took a step back and stared down into her face, his jaw slack with surprise. "My mother knew?"

Chapter Nine

Jace swore under his breath. He wasn't sure how much more he could take. My God. Their baby...his son or daughter...and he'd left Anna alone. She had cared, more than he'd thought possible. And he'd been wrong. So very wrong, and the pain of it nearly brought him to his knees.

"Anna..."

His breath caught at the end of her name and he struggled to keep control. He'd always been angry with her for what he thought she'd done, but he'd always tempered it with his own feelings of guilt on the matter. He'd always felt he'd driven her to it. But now, knowing the truth, he felt about as small as a man could get.

He'd failed her. Utterly and completely. And when her life had fallen apart, she'd still trusted him enough to come to him. He didn't deserve her and he'd endeavor to make it up to her in any way he could.

But to know his own mother had known about the baby...and she'd never said anything. He wasn't sure what to make of that.

"Why didn't she tell me?"

"I asked her not to." Anna wiped her fingers under her eyes. He saw through the darkness, saw that they were red and bruised looking, and again felt the awful guilt that he'd caused it. His mother would never have broken a confidence. He knew that even if it did mean keeping a secret from her own son. They had always been so close, but now there seemed to be a chasm between them. Mom had watched him with a sharp eye that summer, but in the arrogance of youth, he'd ignored her pointed looks. And she'd tried to convince him not to go with Alex. And he'd gone anyway.

He'd failed her too.

"I don't know what to say, Anna. Mom should have said something. I would have been there."

"She tried. She suspected what was happening and tried to keep you from leaving."

He looked away, knowing she was right, hating it.

"Your mama was the closest thing I had to one of my own. When I was a girl becoming a woman, she was the one who talked to me. She taught me what was right. She told me about love. She showed me how to cook and clean and do all the things most women learn to do from their mothers. She made me feel a part of a family, rather than a girl with servants. I never asked her if she knew we'd become intimate, but she certainly understood the day I lost the baby. And still she did not judge me. She held my hand. And when Matteo was born several years later, she came to see me, and I knew she was missing the grandchild she never had a chance to know."

He was shocked. "She said that?"

"She didn't have to," Anna replied quietly. "I think your mother understood a lot of things."

He pictured Mom and Dad with babies. How Dad would enjoy Matteo, showing him how to ride, like he had with Jace. And now Jace had turned his back on something he'd loved, the horses, because it had been more important to beat Roberto Morelli at his own game. And sweet little Aurelia. Mom would dress Aurelia in frills and ruffles and point out the flowers in the garden...

He blinked, desperately trying to clear his vision. His parents deserved more than he'd given them. Mom especially had taken care of Anna when it had been his responsibility.

"My mother," he said in wonderment.

"She is a fine woman. And so very proud of you, Jace. She talks of how you have made life easier for her and for your father."

"We were poor. I just wanted to provide for them. As I wanted to provide for you. When you told me you were pregnant, I knew I couldn't and I ran."

"Your mama was so good to me, Jace. But it was you I really wanted. It was you I missed."

The admission was plain and it was honest and the truth hovered around them. Their feelings, their mistakes, were finally all out in the open, and for the first time they saw each other clearly.

And what he saw was a woman who'd never been quite as privileged as he thought. One who was strong and loving and loyal, in spite of all of her hurts. A woman beautiful in a flowing pale dress, with the moonlight on the curve of her neck and her eyes puffy from crying.

He stepped forward, framed her face with his hands, and kissed her.

She tasted sweet, like the ice wine he'd poured to go with the strawberries for dessert. Her body hovered close to his, and he shifted until his hips grazed her belly and her scent drifted around him, pulling him in.

Gently, he started to release her lips, letting his hands skim down her face, his fingers trail down the soft flesh of her arms. But her lips followed his, asking for more, as goose bumps erupted on her flesh beneath the pads of his fingers.

Don't stop, she seemed to say, and he kept his hands right where he wanted them—touching her. Touching her like he'd wanted to since seeing her again. Touching her like he had all those summers ago. Only now he was no longer a callow youth afraid to explore.

He wanted her. He wanted to show her that what had been between them hadn't been a lie. He wanted a chance to make up for all the mistakes he had made. He wanted to be given a chance to love, not just the girl she had been, but the amazing woman she had become, and he didn't want to just say the words. He'd said the words before and then had made them meaningless. No, this time he would show her with everything nside him. And so he curved her against him and kissed her, over and over, knowing that somehow this would never be enough. Not for them.

Anna clung to his shoulders, and he let feelings crest over him, feelings that he'd held inside for too long. His mouth was on hers, and she tasted exactly the same as she had then, only darker, better. No longer an inexperienced girl but a woman, tall, soft, sexy. Yes, sexy. He wanted to touch all of her, see all of her, possess all of her. She was his and had been even when he'd been so stupid that he'd let her go. Now she was his once more and he'd never let her go again.

He released her and took her hand, saying nothing. To speak would be to break the spell and he didn't want that. He wanted to speak through his actions. There'd been enough talking tonight. Enough apologies and admissions. Now he wanted to start making up for everything.

Her footsteps hurried behind him as he tugged her through the patio doors. The dew on her feet made soft squishing noises on the ceramic tile as they headed for the stairs. They were nearly to his bedroom when he wheeled around, picked her up and carried her over the threshold, using his backside to close the door quietly behind them.

The click of the door echoed in the stillness and he put her down, knowing that finally he had to say one thing.

"Are you sure?"

And then he held his breath.

Anna looked up at him, marveling at how strong and powerful he seemed. Larger than life, and hers. When he'd lifted her in his arms she'd felt young and pretty and so very, very aroused. The anticipation was quivering through her, coming back to her like a long forgotten memory. She hadn't felt like this since the last time they'd made love. Then they'd been sneaking around. Afraid of getting caught.

She caught her bottom lip between her teeth. Now she was just afraid. Her feelings were already expanding, growing, remembering. How did he see her now? She was no longer that innocent girl in the blush of first love. And yet somehow it felt like they deserved this after all they'd shared—and lost.

She remembered the anguish in his voice earlier, and how he'd held her, and she knew that tonight of all nights, she needed him. She needed him to grieve for the baby they'd lost, and she needed him to give credence to the love they'd shared. It *had* been real. One last time in each other's arms felt like the right way to honor it.

She caught the dark, smoldering look in his eyes and felt everything liquefy. "I'm sure. Oh, Jace, I'm so sure. I want you."

He came to her and instantly put his fingers on the zipper to her dress, lowered it in the silence, with only their breathing echoing through the room. His hands, warm and soft, gently lowered the sleeves from the shoulders, the bodice gaping open at the front as he pushed it down to her waist. Once he let it go, it fell off of her slim hips, melting into a puddle around her feet, and leaving her standing in shadow, wearing only her silk panties and bra.

"You are so beautiful." He pressed his lips to her neck and left tiny fires everywhere they touched. A sigh escaped her lips, and then she reached out and began unbuttoning his shirt, button by painstaking button, until the last one was undone and she pushed it off his shoulders.

Their eyes locked. The innocent fumbling of their youth was gone. This was changed, different. More. With a full awareness and yearning.

Before her eyes, he rid himself of the rest of his clothing, came to her naked, and lifted her in his arms.

He placed her on the bed with painstaking gentleness, then stood back to gaze at her. The planes and angles of his body were highlighted by the moonlight coming through the window, and excitement thrummed in her veins. She held out her arms to him, inviting him in. One night could not make up for past wrongs. But it could go a long way in chasing away the pain and disillusionment of the past. He belonged here, with her.

He came to her, bracing his weight on his hands as he covered her body with his, warm and heavy and right. Dipping his head, he sipped from her lips over and over until sensations blended together, making her arch her back as she strained against him. He'd always had a sexual power that had driven her wild, but tonight she was vitally aware Jace was no longer that youth. Now his potency was that of a man. A man who still had the power to light her body on fire. A man whose maturity and strength were even more exciting than before.

"Anna," he whispered hoarsely, sliding to lie beside her, his weight on an elbow while his eyes and hands ravished her body. He undid the fastening at the front of her bra, and her breasts spilled out to his gaze, creamy white in the twilight of his room. His dark gaze met hers, focused, intense, driven. She trembled, realizing she could arouse such passion in him. And when his mouth followed the path of his hands, she shuddered in absolute ecstasy.

His hands were everywhere, touching, tantalizing, until one need overrode everything—the need to feel him inside her.

She nudged him on to his back and slid off her panties. Desire battled briefly with nerves. It had been so long since she'd felt like this, and it was frightening as well as exhilarating. And yet there was a sweet vulnerability that made her turn away from his hot gaze as she slid across the bed and astride him. Taking control had never been something she'd wanted with Stefano. Now, with Jace, she longed to feel the confidence, the seductive power of bringing him to his knees.

She lifted, positioned, and took him in, inch by sweet inch.

She began to move, and she heard Jace swear softly in the darkness. His eyes glittered at her, nearly black, as his hands gripped her hips, urging her on. She watched with satisfaction as his jaw clenched and unclenched and his hips pushed in countermeasure to hers, his breath coming faster as she rocked her hips. Her heart sang as she realized she still had the power to drive him wild.

But victory ceased to matter as sensations built within, insistent, begging for release. She leaned forward, bracing her hands on either side of his head as she ground against him, harder and faster. And when he lifted his head and took her nipple into his mouth, she lost all reason and shattered against him.

Her muscles were still contracting when he grabbed her

hips and plunged deep, finding his own release inside her.

A sound woke him from sleep, and he rolled sluggishly to his side.

The other side of the bed was empty.

For a moment he rolled to his back and stared at the ceiling. It didn't surprise him that she was gone. Things had gotten intense with them...really intense. All the truth coming out in one go had changed things a hundred and eighty degrees. She'd been so torn up, and so had he. And they'd found comfort in each other. Together they'd found a closeness he had never expected.

Only it had been more than comfort, more than shared grief. He ran his hand over his face. Perhaps it had been all of that in the beginning, but it had changed. Right about the time he'd laid her on the coverlet of the bed and had made love to her. Or rather—she had made love to him. His body tightened simply from remembering how she'd slid atop him, shy and seductive. That had been about the here and now.

More than their bodies had been linked. Even he knew that much. And now she was running scared. He couldn't say he blamed her. The reaction was familiar to him. It was the same one he'd made several years earlier. Only he wouldn't let her make the same mistake. They'd both grown since then. There would be no more running away. Whatever needed facing, they'd face together.

There was the sound again. He sat up a little. Perhaps she hadn't gone back to her room. Or maybe she did and she was crying again. She shouldn't have to go through that alone. Not anymore. She was just going to have to get used to the idea that they were in it together.

Silently, he rose from the bed, pulled on his jeans and padded down the hall in search of her.

Matteo's door was closed. She wasn't here. Then the soft sound of her voice reached him, wordless, a soft rise and fall of tones. He tiptoed to the next door and stopped, just out of her line of vision.

Aurelia lay in her arms, her tiny curly-haired head secure in the curve of Anna's neck. Moonlight filtered through the window, highlighting the two of them in its faded beams. Anna now wore a white nightgown, as sweet and innocent as could be, a direct contrast to the red and black underwear she'd worn earlier. The silhouette of her lissome body was visible through the light cotton, her breasts hidden behind the bodice but the delicate curve of her shoulder revealed by the tiny straps. And she was humming softly, her feet and hips moving gently to some song he might have recognized.

Dancing with her baby girl.

Aurelia's lashes fluttered, then settled on her cheeks again, and Jace felt a wave of love crash over him. His girls. Somehow, in just this short amount of time, they had become his girls. He had loved Anna half his life and had spent a great deal of that time resenting her, or at least convincing himself he should to make his mistakes hurt less. But now she was his. Tonight had proved that. Now he knew the truth, and he could go about making things right. And Aurelia—she was an angel. Holding her in his arms the day she'd been stung had awakened something in him. A protectiveness he hadn't expected. All she had to do was turn her toothy grin on him and he was a goner.

He'd do right by them all. And if that meant trading in his Porsche in return for stepping in and doing what was right for these children, he'd do it gladly. He'd see Two Willows flourish, and he'd provide for them. They would want for nothing.

Her bare feet made tiny circles and his pulse quickened. His Anna. They would put the past behind them and she would see this was where she belonged.

He stepped into the room, and she turned, startled at his sudden presence.

"Is she asleep?" he whispered.

"I think so." Anna tried to keep her voice steady and failed. He looked so sexy standing there in the gray moonlight, with just his jeans on and no shirt, no shoes. She realized the jeans were unbuttoned and that he wore nothing beneath them and she blushed, turned away and placed Aurelia very gently back in the playpen, covering her with a blanket.

But that didn't work either, for when she turned around again he was still there, and now her hands were unoccupied. She knew exactly where she wanted to put them.

And she knew it would be a big mistake.

She'd heard Aurelia's whimpers and she'd gone to her, tended to her, the moment in the shadows bittersweet as she had thought about the baby she'd never known. She and Jace could not turn back the clock or change what had happened. She closed her eyes briefly. These moments with him were not real. They were a reaction, a reaction that had been long years in coming. She had to keep looking forward. She had to remember her goals. And Jace's way of life still did not fit with what she wanted. What she needed.

But it was so very difficult to remember when he stood before her, warm and sexy and wanting her. Harder still knowing how much she wanted him.

"Come back to bed," he suggested softly.

The very idea was so seductive she nearly followed him to the door. But she paused. The fire that had burned between them tonight couldn't be sustained in the clear light of day.

Emotions were at a peak, but she was smart enough to know they were a reaction to something that had happened nearly a decade before. Tonight had all the earmarks of a huge mistake and she didn't need to make it again.

"I should be here if she wakes up again."

"My room is just down the hall. You heard her the first time, didn't you?"

His hushed whispers caused the baby to stir and Anna knew they had to talk outside the room. Only that meant they would be one step closer to his bedroom. Damn.

She pulled the door mostly shut behind her. "She's used to sleeping with me, Jace."

"I can see how she wouldn't want to give that up," he said, a charming smile quirking the corner of his mouth. He reached out and tucked a piece of hair behind her ear. "In the moonlight just now, in that nightgown, you looked like an angel, Anna."

She swallowed. She'd picked the plainest cotton thing she could find, hoping to somehow regain her balance. Didn't men like silk and lace? He'd certainly approved of her underwear earlier. "You are all flattery."

"No," he responded. His body was close and she backed up, only the wall was behind her and there was no place to go. She could feel the warmth of his chest against her even though they weren't touching. "Tonight is about only truth. And the truth is you're the most beautiful woman I've ever seen. Ever touched. Ever loved."

He leaned in, putting his hands on the wall on either side of her head. The heat from his body was like a magnet, and everything in her stuttered.

"Come back to bed with me," he whispered. His breath was in her ear and her whole body shivered in response. She wanted to. If this wasn't real, was there truly any harm in letting it last

147

a few more hours? Maybe that would be enough, for both of them. Perhaps tomorrow was time enough to think clearly. If this was all she would let herself have, shouldn't she have all of it? They were older now. It didn't matter about his intentions. She knew Jace now as a man. He wasn't interested in marriage. And for one night, she wanted to feel like a desirable woman. She hadn't felt like anything beyond a failure for so long.

She wanted to feel loved by the man who knew her best. Maybe it was selfish. She knew the children came first. But she'd spent so many years doing the right thing that this one night she wanted to break her own rules and do something one hundred percent indulgent.

He moved one hand from the wall, and a long finger stroked up her arm, down her collarbone to graze the side of her breast. Her skin fluttered and goose bumps erupted over her body.

"Yes," she whispered, and he took her hand. And when they reached his room, he shut the door.

Anna left him sleeping and tiptoed to the door. She had to creep into her bedroom and dress before the children were up and demanding breakfast. Already the sun was higher than it normally was when she woke, and it wouldn't do for Matteo to catch her in Jace's room. She was determined to set a better example than his father had. Stefano's affair had changed everything. She did not want to confuse Matteo further.

Today she had to step out into the light and decide what came next. Not just for her. But for all of them. And what had to come first was the happiness of her children.

The day was already hot. Aurelia slept fitfully as Anna pulled on her clothes. She'd wake any time. Aurelia's rising in the middle of the night must have caused her to sleep longer than normal. She dressed in denim capris and a sleeveless top and then checked Matteo's room. He was sitting on his bed with a bag of marbles, arranging them in a circle, with the colored ones on the inside.

"Good morning," she said lightly, sticking her head in the door. "Are you hungry? Get dressed and I'll make you breakfast."

"Are we going in the boat today?"

This was the problem with toys. Until the novelty wore off, he would keep nagging to enjoy it.

"Not today. We need to work, both Jace and me. You and Aurelia can come with me and play with your toys at the guesthouse."

His lips set. Clearly he didn't like that idea.

"Come, Matteo, I'll make Francesca's frittatas. And maybe after our work is done, we can go for a swim."

"But you don't like swimming."

She stepped in the room. "I used to swim all the time." She smiled a little. Indeed. "Did you know that Jace and I used to swim in a stream very close to *Nonno* Roberto's house?" She didn't add that many a time it was without benefit of a swimsuit. They'd been young and foolish and so sure they were bulletproof.

"Will Jace go with us?"

"Go with you where?"

She jumped at the sound of his voice. When she turned she saw he had a very awake, very quiet Aurelia in his arms. The arms that had held her and loved her most of the night. His golf shirt hugged his form, strong and dark against the pale delicateness of the baby's skin.

"Swimming," Matteo answered, oblivious to anything

happening between his mother and Jace.

"What did your mama say?"

"I have to get dressed and have frittata and that you have to work and maybe later."

Jace laughed, the warm masculine sound sending shivers down the backs of her legs. Oh, this wouldn't do at all.

"That sounds fair to me. I'm going to be out in the vines all day. A swim will feel good tonight, though."

"Okay."

Jace nodded. "But you have to be good for your mama, you hear?"

"Yes, sir." Matteo agreed instantly, respectfully, and Anna stilled.

What had she done?

They had needed to talk. And she was glad the truth was out. But what was said—and done—in the dark last night was very, very different in the clear light of day. He was starting to step in, in small insidious ways. First with the boat and with Aurelia and now giving instructions. She wasn't sure she wanted that. Not that Jace had done anything wrong, but she didn't want Matteo especially to get his feelings pinned on Jace. He'd already lost one male figure, albeit a mediocre-to-poor one. But to let him rely on Jace and take him away again...and take him she knew she must. This was a place to heal and regroup, but not to start over. Their future was not here. She had a house and a job in Victoria. Matteo would be more confused. And hurt.

She hadn't foreseen this happening. And perhaps she should have, but she'd been thinking in crisis mode, and the idea that Matteo and Jace would bond hadn't crossed her mind. Especially after the way they had crossed swords the first night.

"I'll take Aurelia. She needs to be changed. And then I'll make us all breakfast, okay?"

She couldn't meet his eyes. Instead she focused on the baby, forcing a smile where she felt none. Sleeping with Jace had been a mistake. She'd suspected it at the time but had ignored the warnings. Guilt slid through her. Once again, she'd made a choice based on her own wants and not the bigger picture.

It had been beautiful but a mistake nonetheless. It should have been about ending something that had never truly been ended. She wanted to build her own life for herself and for her children. The last thing she'd wanted was to find herself smack dab in the middle of...whatever it was they were. Clearly not over, if Jace's actions were any indication.

Jace stepped back as she took Aurelia from his arms, and she sensed the cautiously confused look on his face. She would explain it later, when the children were occupied.

After breakfast he disappeared, and she determinedly cleaned up the mess and packed up the children. The day was sunny and warm again, and she made sure they were set up with lots of toys before going inside and taping off the living room, preparing it for the paint she'd chosen.

She took frequent breaks to check on Matteo and Aurelia, read them stories and unwrapped snacks. This was what she'd wanted all along. Freedom. She could spend her time the way she wanted, yet inside she was making progress, on her own schedule, and it gave her such a sense of accomplishment. How long since she'd known such freedom? Perhaps never. There had always been some expectation at the Morelli office, or a standard to uphold as Stefano's wife. She was tired of it and had come here wanting to find out how to define herself.

She sighed. She hadn't meant to define herself by attaching

herself to Jace again. Wouldn't that be a step backwards? Oh, trying to make sense of it all only confused her more.

"Mama?"

She paused, her paint roller in hand, at Matteo's tiny voice.

"Yes, darling?"

"We're tired."

"Would you like to sleep on the bed upstairs for a while?"

He nodded, and she smiled softly, putting the roller back in the tray and going over to hug him close. "Lots of playing and fresh air," she said. "Let's get Aurelia changed."

She gave Aurelia a bottle and tucked them both under a light blanket, the baby already asleep on the wall side of the bed and Matteo's eyes heavy as he curled up beside her. She wondered briefly what their baby would have looked like, hers and Jace's. Dark hair surely. And brown eyes. And a hint of dimples, like their daddy. Sadness mixed with tenderness as she ran one gentle finger over Matteo's cheek. She'd thought telling Jace would end these feelings, but now wondered if they would ever go away. Or if she wanted them to. In some way, it kept her heart tethered to his.

She left the children there and went to finish the primer coat on the wall. She was washing out the roller at the kitchen sink when Jace came in.

"You planning on staying all day?"

She smiled, trying to push down the sense of excitement she felt just knowing he was close by. He came into the kitchen, a bag in his hands and a grin on his face.

"That was the plan. I'm painting the living room today."

He held out the bag. "And Matteo and Aurelia?"

"Tired out. Asleep upstairs."

"So we are alone."

Her heart tripped as he said exactly what she was thinking. "Yes."

He flashed a quicksilver smile. "Perfect." He put the bag on the countertop and stepped forward, pressing a kiss to her surprised lips.

"Jace," she chided, but he simply laughed, put his arms around her and kissed her again.

And oh, he tasted good. So good she could have kissed him here in the kitchen all afternoon long. For a few moments, she let herself go and kissed him back. But in the end she made herself push away. She couldn't get carried away again. Yesterday had been different. Today had to be about clearer heads.

Her cheeks flushed, she looked at the plastic bag instead of him. "What's in there?"

"Lemonade." He reached in and pulled out a glass bottle. "It's a hot day. I thought everyone might enjoy it."

"It's lovely, but you don't have to take care of us, Jace." She put the bottle on the counter and rinsed a few glasses from the cupboard, just to keep her hands busy.

"I know. I want to."

Were they still talking about lemonade? She wasn't sure. It was a small gesture and a lovely one, but there was more going on here.

All day she had been thinking about what to do, and she'd come up with a pseudo plan. They couldn't stay here. They would all come to rely on Jace too much. She'd come to regroup and she was doing that. Talking to Jace yesterday had been painful, but it had helped put some of the unresolved issues between them to rest. It had cleared the air of so many of the things they should have talked about sooner. The past was behind them. She needed to move on. And she needed to do it standing on her own two feet, not by jumping into another dependent situation. That's exactly what would happen if she stayed here with Jace.

"Speaking of, there's something else in the bag. But it's just for you."

She reached in and pulled out a small rectangular box. Her heart froze. Surely he didn't feel the need to ply her with gifts after they'd made love. The lemonade soured in her mouth. It was something Stefano had done in the past, given her something from the jewelers when she'd pleased him in some way.

It wasn't that she wanted anything from Jace, she didn't. And she definitely didn't want a lover's token to cheapen what had been between them.

With trembling fingers, she opened it. It was a twisted silver chain with the most gorgeous locket she had ever seen. The heart shape was over an inch high, and stamped in the middle was an orchid. One that looked just like the orchid on the Morelli logo.

It was too much, and her throat clogged, not at the beauty of the piece, but at the gesture. Didn't he realize his welcoming kiss meant just as much? It only proved that she was right in deciding to move on.

"How did you...I mean, where did you find this today? You cannot convince me this piece was in the village. And you haven't had time to travel elsewhere or have anything shipped."

He came to her and clasped her hand, so that the necklace was held by the two of them. "Of course not. I have had this a long time."

She didn't understand. "But we have been over for..."

"Forever," he finished. He pressed the gentlest of kisses on the crest of her cheek. "You don't see, do you?"

She shook her head. When she'd picked up the box she'd been afraid it was a lover's morning-after gift. But now it dawned on her that it was so much more, and her insides twisted with a combination of elation and fear. This made it so much worse.

"I bought this in Vancouver. I had to borrow the money from Alex back then. We were on our way home. I wanted to buy you a ring but knew I couldn't afford it. But this...I wanted to give it to you when I proposed. I thought..."

He broke off, cleared his throat. "Alex didn't know. He thought I was off to buy something for my mom's birthday. But I saw the orchid and thought of you. I knew the story behind your family, you see. How your grandmother was the one with the fortune and your grandfather was the poor boy, but how it was their love that made them strong. I wasn't totally blind, Anna. And I thought you could put a picture of our baby inside."

When had he become so sentimental?

And didn't he know how much it hurt to receive such a gift now? Now, when any possibility of putting a picture inside was gone?

"Why now?" she whispered, touching the orchid on the front with the tip of her finger.

"I don't know," he answered softly. "It seemed right. Considering all that happened yesterday. Considering how far we've come."

But had they come so far? All they'd done was finally have a conversation they should have had—and had avoided—for too many years. And making love had been... Her body flushed all over. It had been incredible. More than incredible. But it had been a reaction, and she was no longer foolish enough to make big decisions based on an emotional reaction. She'd done that before and had ended up married to Stefano.

This time she had to keep her eye on the big picture. And this time it wasn't only her heart at stake. It was the lives of her children. She was too old and wise now to take risks.

"I'm sorry, Jace. I don't think I should accept this."

She pulled her hand away and put the chain back in the box. But when she moved to hand it back to him, he held up his hands.

"No, Anna. It is yours. It has always been yours. What you choose to do with it, I'll leave to you."

"I don't want you to think I need presents."

His chin flattened. She got the impression she'd insulted him, but that hadn't been her intention. She just didn't want him to think there was more to this than there was.

"Perhaps I *wanted* to give it to you."

She didn't want to fight over it. She didn't want to fight with him at all anymore. Now was as good a time as any to tell him what she'd decided while she was rolling paint today. She took a deep breath, hoping he wouldn't interrupt midstream so she could get it all out. Make him understand, without there being hard feelings. They'd already had enough hard feelings for a lifetime.

"Look, Jace, I'm very glad we talked. We should have a long time ago and it feels...good knowing it is not between us anymore. But yesterday...it was simply a reaction to something we should have resolved and didn't. Closing a chapter, do you see?"

His jaw clenched, and she quailed a little but knew she had to press on. She had to finish this job to put the rest into motion. But it wouldn't do to lead him on.

"I've been thinking. And once everything is delivered and in place next week, the children and I are leaving."

"Leaving." A muscle in his jaw ticked, and his eyes darkened. "Where are you going?"

She lifted her chin. She could do this, she could. "I want to branch out on my own. The one thing I loved about my home was the ability to decorate it the way I wanted. And I've really enjoyed putting together your guesthouse. I'm going to take some courses and then build my own business as a decorator. I've been doing marketing for Morelli, so the business side will be a breeze. I've really enjoyed the hands-on part here. I can take my time and decide what to do about my house and Morelli. But building something new, it's what's right. For me and for the children."

"You're running away."

She shook her head. "No, Jace. Running away was what I did when I came here, and I came here to figure things out. I've come to realize a lot of things. And one is I need to look forward and make a life for me, and Matteo and Aurelia. I'm not running. I just refuse to make huge life decisions based on emotion, which is what I did when I lost the baby." She took a breath and forged forward. "It was what I did last night. I let my emotions rule my head. From now on, I'm thinking things through."

She met his eyes and just said the words. "The children and I will be leaving for the Island next Friday."

A cry sounded from the doorway and they both turned their heads. Matteo stood in the breach, his brown eyes flashing and his lips set in a hateful line.

"No! I do not want to go!" He shouted it right at his mother. "*I hate you!*"

"Matteo!" Anna gasped at the outburst, but Matteo spun and ran out the front door, slamming it behind him. The bang woke Aurelia, who immediately started crying.

Jace gave Anna a withering glare. "You get Aurelia. I'll find Matteo."

He left her in the kitchen, making her feel like the world's worst parent all over again.

Chapter Ten

Matteo's tiny legs couldn't compete with Jace's long ones. He caught up with the boy when he was only halfway across the yard. Neither were the kicks and furious grunts aimed at him any match for Jace's strength. He simply scooped up the boy and held on until he quieted.

"I'm sorry, Matteo."

He looked down into the brown eyes, recognizing the confusion and upset reflected there. He meant so much more by the words than Matteo would ever understand. But he was smart enough to know that Matteo was hurting and was at an age where he couldn't possibly make sense of it. Hell, Jace didn't even understand and he had thirty more years of experience.

Matteo stuck out his lip. "Why are *you* sorry?"

Jace refused to look away. "I'm sorry because you lost your papa and now your mama says you are leaving again. That is why you're angry, yes?"

"Put me down. Please."

The last word was the only reason Jace complied.

"Jace?"

"Yes, Matteo."

"I am going to miss your boat."

Jace tried not to laugh. Matteo was so clear, so honest in what he wanted. Growing up complicated things. He took Matteo's hand, the smaller size unfamiliar but not unwelcome in his own. He gripped it tightly, hoping he could reassure the boy. Had it only been a few weeks ago that he'd resisted having the children here? And now he could hardly imagine Two Willows without them. "You are not gone yet. We'll still go for rides. I promise."

He wished he could convince Anna to stay as easily as he'd gotten through to Matteo. Surely she had to see their mistakes could be righted. This didn't have to mark an ending. It could be a beginning. He could provide for her now. He'd given her the locket as an attempt to begin proving it. But perhaps she needed more incentive. He looked around him as the sun glowed warmly on the exterior of the guesthouse. Two Willows was a wonderful place to raise a family. He could offer her that. She had to see how happy her children were, with the trees and grass and the water surrounding them. He could buy a few horses, show Matteo all those things his father had shown him as a boy. The things he had enjoyed with Anna and Alex as they'd grown. Now he could provide that and so much more.

All he knew was that this time he wasn't going to give up so easily.

"Let me talk to your mama about it," he said, kneeling before Matteo. "For right now I don't want you to worry. Why don't we go for that swim I promised?"

Matteo's eyes suddenly swam with tears.

"What is wrong now?"

"You said I had to be good for Mama." A sniffle cut the sentence from the next one. "I wasn't good. I said I hated her."

Ah. Again Jace bit back a smile. He was beginning to understand why Anna tried so hard. Matteo's soulful eyes stared up at him, seeking some sort of absolution, and Jace meant to give it.

"Did you mean it?"

He shook his head.

"You were angry?"

Matteo shrugged and Jace's heart softened further. "Maybe scared?"

Another shrug.

Anna came out of the guesthouse with Aurelia on her hip. His heart caught, tangled up in wishes that somehow their child could have lived. She was such a good mother, and at first it had surprised him. But not now. Anna had a world of love in her heart, but for right now it was reserved only for her children. What would it take to break down the walls around it, so she could love him too?

Jace stood, holding Matteo's small hand in his. She paused and stared at him, her with the baby in her arms and him with her son holding his hand. He'd be damned if he'd let her get away this time. But he couldn't press his case. Not with the children listening to every word. She'd already said how Matteo had heard her arguing with Stefano. No, this was something they had to do alone. Right now they had to do something to cool the tension simmering.

She came forward and he forced the muscles in his body to relax. "Is she okay?"

"She was just scared."

Aurelia had her fingers in her mouth, but as Jace reached out and smoothed her curls, she let go and reached out for him. "Up," she said.

Jace let go of Matteo's hand and took her into his arms. He settled her comfortably, absurdly pleased by the confounded look on Anna's face. "I think Matteo wants to say something," he prodded. He put his free hand on Matteo's head, encouraging, supporting.

Matteo scuffed the ground with a toe, reverting to the Italian he had learned at home. "*Mi dispiace.* I'm sorry, Mama. *Ti amo.*"

She knelt before him. "And I love you. Always."

He hugged her then and she turned her eyes up at Jace as Matteo's arms clasped her neck. It was clear to him she wasn't sure how they'd gotten to this point. And no matter what she said, she *was* running scared and making decisions based on that emotion. It was also equally clear to him the cause. His chest swelled as the impact struck, and he knew more than ever that he couldn't give up.

She still loved him. And he loved her. Always had. It had always been between them, an alive, breathing thing, only made dormant in the intervening years. Now, suddenly awakened, it was more powerful than ever. It had been awakened last night and acknowledged during their lovemaking.

He imagined it was a lot for her to process. He wished he could go slowly, take his time to convince her. But he only had a week...and she was prepared to fight him every step of the way. He could tell by the way she kept her hands away from his. Careful not to touch.

"I told Matteo we could go swimming."

"That's a good idea."

It surprised him that she agreed, but perhaps they both understood the need for a distraction. "If you'll get them ready—"

"Jace, I—"

"Not now." His voice was low with warning. He had much to

say, but not in front of the children.

"I'll meet you under the willow in ten minutes." He spoke to Matteo but meant it for Anna.

Anna finished folding the laundry and sighed. It would be so easy to stay, but what then? She put the tiny pajamas on top of the pile and rested her hand on the soft cotton. She wasn't stupid. There was a lot between her and Jace. And she loved him. She loved him perhaps as much as she had as a girl. Maybe even more.

Which meant nothing had changed. And she desperately needed it to change. She needed to break the pattern. Loving Jace had broken her heart and she wasn't sure she could survive that again. It had led to her knee-jerk reaction of marrying Stefano, another huge mistake. She did not regret her children, but she did regret the choices she'd made that had brought them all to this place.

She closed her eyes, trying to drive away the memory of his sheets on her skin, the warmth of him beside her. This had all happened because of a reaction to the past. It was flawed logic and when the fog cleared, who would pay the price? Matteo and Aurelia. Jace would realize he didn't want the family package and they would be left again. Only this time it would be worse. This time there wouldn't be any comfort in blame. She put her hand in her pocket and felt the locket resting there, warm against her skin. What it represented frightened her. She didn't want his promises, not when she was so afraid he'd only break them. The thought of letting herself love him again and possibly losing him made it hard for her to breathe.

She wished she could think of a way to make him understand that without starting another argument.

The laundry completed and the children asleep, she

decided she needed a walk. Slipping on her sandals, she tiptoed down the stairs and out the door, seeking the solace and privacy of the river.

It was nearly dark when Jace looked out of his bedroom window and saw Anna beneath the curtain of the willow, leaning against the trunk, her head resting against the gnarly bark. She looked lonely. She looked very much as he'd felt since relocating here. For so long he'd wondered if he'd made a mistake buying the winery here instead of closer to home. He had chosen the Similkameen Valley because being close to Morelli was too much of a reminder. But he'd missed his family. He'd missed the companionship in the evenings, someone to share a table and a good-natured teasing with. Anna and her children had changed that in such a small space of time. They made Two Willows feel like home.

In his bare feet, he stepped through the cool grass until he reached the tree.

"Anna?"

"Oh." Anna hadn't heard him approach, and hastily she ran her fingers under her eyes. She didn't want him to see her crying, didn't want him to know he was the cause of it.

"We need to talk. About what happened last night. About what will happen now."

"Do we have to?"

"I think so, yes."

He ducked under the green curtain and put his hands in his pockets. Anna sat, leaned her back against the trunk of the tree and crossed her legs at the knees. Her hair was still damp from the swim in the water with Aurelia. There had been times when Jace had caught her gaze and she'd known he was thinking about what she'd told him about the water just yesterday. As the children had splashed, Anna and Jace had been unusually quiet. All that time, this moment had lain ahead of them. And now it was here, and she didn't know what to say.

"Matteo is having difficulty understanding." He spoke first.

She nodded. It was surprising that his first thought would be for Matteo, especially when the two of them had butted heads so early on. It was a safer topic than discussing herself, but it was also a reminder of how involved Jace already was in their lives. Another reason why it was better to make the change now.

"There has been a lot for him to digest, and he is confused. I didn't realize he'd get so attached to being here. I hate that I have to hurt him again."

"So don't. Stay."

The fact he was even asking sent a hidden thrill through her, but she pushed it away with logic. She wouldn't settle for anything less than permanence, and she didn't quite believe in anything permanent from Jace. Oh, he'd mean it for now, but parenthood wasn't a few weeks in the summer at a winery. To pretend otherwise, to follow wherever it led would only hurt them all.

"You are fooling yourself, thinking we can start over. Too much has passed. It's why I cannot possibly accept your gift."

"Why am I fooling myself? I was there last night. I felt you in my arms. That was not pretending."

She considered, sighed and stared out over the river. "Yes, it was. It was pretending nothing had changed. It was acting on impulse. Impulses are exactly what destroyed us in the first place."

"Just don't rush, Anna. Stay for a while. Give us time to make a decision. Think about the possibility."

"Until when? We both know it is only a matter of time and you'll get tired of this competition with my father. You'll hire a manager and only be here a few times a year while you do something else. There is no possibility."

She stared off into the distance at the ripples in the river, yet not truly seeing anything at all. Instead, her mind was full of images of Jace last night. His hands on her face just before he kissed her. The look of anguish in his eyes as she told him about their baby. And the way his soul had reached out and touched hers as they'd made love in the shadows of his room.

"Too many attachments have been made. If we prolong it, it will hurt more in the end. My children have been hurt enough. If I go now, they will not remember."

"This isn't about the children. And it sure as hell isn't about your father. When did I ever give the impression that Two Willows was temporary?"

"You've always moved around."

"I was learning. And looking."

"For what?" She furrowed her brow, suddenly unsure. Even Alex had expressed concern at Jace's wandering ways over the years. But what if they'd been wrong?

"For home," he replied simply. "I thought I'd found a home."

She turned away. He thought his words spoke volumes, but he didn't offer any guarantees. He never had.

"This is about you," he said. "And this is about you not trusting me. I didn't trust you. I was a coward. I ran when it got difficult. And you didn't trust me then either. You didn't wait to see if I'd come back. Instead you rushed into marriage. One would hope we have grown since. That we have learned *something.*"

She closed her eyes. She wanted to give in so badly it physically hurt, but she had done that once. She'd let herself love him with all her heart even knowing he wasn't ready for it. It had nearly broken her in the end. She couldn't do it again, and she couldn't drag the children along with her. A woman's heart could only take a beating so often.

"Maybe it is about me," she acquiesced quietly. "Once, I trusted you. I loved you. I gave you everything. And you walked away."

"I'm different now."

"How?" *Convince me.*

He turned sideways, taking her hand in his. "I can provide for you now. I can provide for you all. I can give you a good life. The life you have always deserved."

Tears stung the backs of her eyes. She didn't give a good damn about his money. She had money of her own. This wasn't about trusting him with her checkbook. It was about her heart, and the hearts of her children.

"You haven't changed at all, Jace. You still don't get it."

He stiffened. "I am still not good enough for you, is that it?"

She watched him soberly. "That is you talking, not me. You were always the one hung up on status and bank balances. I have never said you were not good enough for me. Not once. Until now."

"What the hell is that supposed to mean?"

"It means you do not understand what I want any more now than you did then." She pulled her hand out of his grasp. "I have been 'taken care of' my whole life. First by my father and Alex, and then Stefano. On the outside Stefano and I had a fine life. I had everything I could ever want. I had a husband who cared nothing for me beyond my connection to Morelli, and who thought so little of me as a woman that he had an affair with our nanny.

"I don't want that kind of love. I want to stand on my own two feet. I can look after myself. I do not need money. I have enough of my own. I certainly didn't come here looking to get swept off my feet, or to fall into some situation where someone 'looks after me' again."

Her stomach tumbled as the words rolled off her tongue. Swept was exactly what he'd done last night. And he was right about one thing, it scared the living hell out of her. "I'm glad we talked, because finally it's out in the open and we can put it behind us. But I'm not here to repeat past mistakes. Now I can start a new life. A good life." She put her hands on her hips. "A life on *my* terms."

"Your children need a father."

Oh, how she agreed. And seeing the way Matteo had warmed to Jace only drove the matter home. But it was precisely why they had to go now, before the attachment grew even stronger. Matteo would not understand. "They had a father, and that didn't work out so well. And now they have me. I won't be pushed into something out of guilt for the situation I find myself in. I got in it. I'm now out of it and I'm going to make sure I stay that way."

Oh God, she'd come here so sure she could never love again, knowing that because of it she could put Matteo and Aurelia first. Now she was as deeply involved as she'd ever been and her longing was warring with doing what was right. What kind of a mother did that make her? She couldn't put herself first. She'd done that all along. So even though she longed to give in, she pushed the idea away.

"And I'm one of those mistakes." There was a dangerous

edge to his voice, but she wasn't afraid of him anymore. She was far more afraid of herself and of giving into what she knew would be a terrible error in judgment. He was speaking from guilt about the past. He wasn't making rational decisions, and right now one of them had to.

"The time for looking backwards is past. That's all this is. Us finally coming to terms with something that happened long ago. We're older now, wiser. We're not impulsive teenagers anymore. I'm looking forward, and right now that means going home. Setting up my business and loving Matteo and Aurelia. Let me do that, Jace. For the sake of our friendship and for the sake of my children."

She started to walk away. It would be so easy to give in and love *him*, just for now. It was only the fear of losing herself again that kept her feet moving one step in front of the other.

"This time who is the coward?"

His voice was pure acid aimed at her back, and it burned. But she kept walking, all the way to the house, all the way to the bedroom, where she closed the door behind her.

For Jace, the following week was a disaster. First of all, it rained a good portion of the time and the children were fractious. There were no moments alone in which Jace and Anna could talk, try to work things out. Opportunities to press his case, make her see sense, never seemed to arise. Anna took the children to the guesthouse and worked with them there, supervising deliveries of new furniture and hanging drapes. Every time a truck drove in to the yard, he gritted his teeth. Every successful change was one closer to her leaving, and he had no idea how to convince Anna to stay. He countered each move with one of his own, but it seemed to get him nowhere. He didn't know what she wanted from him. He was prepared to give her everything he had, and she handed it back to him as though it were dirty.

She had to see that he was committed. He took a precious day and went to Kamloops, coming back without the Porsche but with a vehicle that looked like a cross between a car and a truck and had seats that could flip up to seat extra passengers. When she'd questioned him about it, he had stated that it seemed more practical than a sports car. He came in from a long day on Wednesday and then took Matteo out in the boat despite his fatigue. She wanted him to show her, and he was trying to do that.

Then there was a crisis at the Two Willows vineyard in Osoyoos and he had to drive down to oversee it. Two more days lost, two days he could not be there to see her, talk to her.

Finally, on Thursday, he drove up the 97 and made his way home. All he could think of was that tomorrow she could be making this drive going the other direction. And if he lost her this time, she'd be gone for good.

He turned the car into the drive. For some reason it felt, for the first time, like coming home. The sun was deepening its shadows and as he got out of the driver's side, he could hear mourning doves down over the hill.

And then he saw her car with the trunk open and a single suitcase already inside.

Fear struck his heart, replaced almost immediately with anger that she was in such a hurry to depart. Was he that much of a threat? Did she find being near him so very repulsive? Did his efforts mean nothing to her?

At that moment she stepped out of the house with a bag on her shoulder and he froze.

She did too, for a moment. He could have sworn she looked

guilty. Was she planning on sneaking out before his return? Maybe leaving a note and not saying goodbye? Bitterness burned hotly in his veins. And she had the nerve to call him a coward. It appeared she couldn't get away fast enough.

"Going somewhere?"

She pasted on a smile, but he saw through it.

"It takes a while to pack for three. I don't want to be rushed in the morning."

"Right." He started walking towards her, saw the flare of panic in her eyes and took pleasure in it. "Where are you going?"

"Home to Papa's, for now."

"I see."

He paused in front of her and noticed her hand was fidgeting, holding the bag. She lifted her chin a little. "Did you want to see the guesthouse? It's done, and I'm quite pleased with how it turned out."

"I don't give a damn about the guesthouse," he said pleasantly, the amiable tone a threat in itself.

"You don't—"

"That's right."

"But that was our deal, so you could expand, open it up for tourists, build Two Willows."

He stepped up onto the verandah beside her and stared into her wide eyes. She genuinely looked confused. He wasn't sure how someone so smart and savvy could be so completely blind.

"It was your idea, not mine. I went along with it because it was sensible and it gave you a purpose, and I knew you needed it. But you finishing is not why you're leaving, so don't pretend it is. You, Anna Morelli, are a first-class deceiver. Too bad the one you're deceiving is yourself."

He strode past her, inside, wanting to see Matteo and Aurelia before she took them away. But the slam of the door told him he'd struck a nerve.

"What is that supposed to mean?"

She stood at the threshold of the kitchen, eyes blazing. Was she actually insulted?

"It means that you are running away, and I don't care what you say or how you defend it, that's the truth. What was between us...what is between us, has got you so terrified you can't get away fast enough. And you can turn it all on me if you want, but it's not me. Or at least it's not just me. It's you, Anna. I've tried to tell you in every way I can, and I've tried to show you how much...how I want you to stay. I got rid of the car you called my 'toy' when you arrived. I spend time with your children and I do little things. Why do you think that is? You told me words weren't enough. Well, you're all packed and it's made me see that maybe nothing I do will ever be enough. It's just easier to blame me than to take a good long look in the mirror."

The bag dropped to the floor and he tried to ignore the sharp stabs of guilt as her eyes filled with tears.

"That is the cruelest thing you have ever said to me." Her voice was little more than a whisper.

"It's the truth." He was unrelenting, but if he didn't say it now, when could he? Tomorrow she'd be leaving him for good. "And if you're leaving anyway, maybe it's time for a little truth. The truth is you made a mistake in marrying Stefano. You didn't wait before writing me off. You never felt the need to tell me about our baby, you just let me assume what had happened. You knew who I was, what I was, and made sure you married someone completely opposite. And when it all fell apart,

172

you came to me anyway. Because you knew I could not say no to you."

"That makes me sound horrible, like some opportunist. That's not how it was." Her words were choked with tears.

But Jace had held things in for years as well, and he'd somehow hoped that she would change her mind about leaving. Instead she was already packed and he could still smell the memory of her scent, still feel her touch, even when she wasn't present. And he was hurt, dammit.

"It's exactly how it was. You laid the truth on me, and you made love with me, and then you tossed me aside. And you call me cruel," he scoffed.

"Jace, please." It was a begging whisper.

But there was no stopping him now. "You let me care. You let me hope. You brought your children into my life and now you are leaving it again."

"You don't even like children."

"How do you know, Anna? Have you ever asked what I wanted? Or has it always been about you?"

Her eyes widened and he thought for a moment he'd gotten through to her.

"You said so, that day by the stream when I told you I was pregnant."

"That was years ago!"

He clenched his fingers into tight balls. She understood nothing. He had told her he'd come back to marry her and still she couldn't move past the one reaction he'd had at the news. It was over, he realized. He had offered her all he could think to give, and she had turned it away. She would always judge him by that moment.

He was suddenly so very, very tired. Like a decade's worth

of fatigue had caught up with him and left him reeling. He thought briefly of Matteo's brown eyes begging for a boat ride and Aurelia's chubby arms reaching out as she said "Up." And he exhaled slowly, knowing it was all slipping away from him, only to be replaced by the knowledge that he'd failed, yet again, even more spectacularly than the first time.

"Just go," he murmured, pushing past her and back out into the yard before she could see exactly what she'd done to him.

Anna covered her mouth with her hands and let the tears come.

Jace had been her rock, her safe place. She'd told herself for many years that it wasn't meant to be, and she'd tried not to hate him for leaving her. She'd put it aside for the sake of friendship. It was a shock to realize he held so many of his own resentments. She blamed herself for so much already. But knowing she'd let him down, seeing the pain and hatred on his face, it weighed far heavier than anything she'd come up against so far.

She went out to the deck, wiping her eyes, but still the tears came, hot and fast. Her knees shook and she sat on one of the deck chairs. She had no idea he thought so little of her.

He was her champion, but now she was realizing she hadn't lived up to earning him.

He was right. She hadn't waited, and she'd regretted it since. But she'd justified it by telling herself over and over that if only he hadn't gone with Alex...that he had driven her to it. This summer she had let him close, they had talked about the baby and grieved together, and she'd been a willing participant in their night together. She'd brought her children here, and it was clear to anyone who bothered to look that Matteo and Aurelia adored him. And she'd told herself he didn't like children based on their first few days at Two Willows, rather than all the times he had doted on them.

She had seen what she wanted to.

And she had hurt him.

Her heart ached knowing it. And yet, he still thought that the way to her heart was to buy his way in. The reason he'd gone in the first place was because he'd said he couldn't give her the life she deserved. And now he said he could, but she didn't want material riches. In the end they were just things. He mentioned the car and the children but not once had he said he loved her. Not once had it come down to that one common denominator; what was in their hearts. She had laid hers on the line for him once before. She inhaled and squared her shoulders. Was it so unreasonable that she was afraid to do it again?

All she wanted, the only security she craved, was knowing she was loved by him, that he would stand beside her no matter what. And his last words to her were, "Just go".

Congratulations, Anna, she told herself. She'd done the exact opposite of what she'd set out to do.

She'd lost her champion after all.

Chapter Eleven

Jace stalked down the path towards the river, away from the house, away from her. Despite his last words, he didn't want to give up. He didn't know how to give up, yet he had no idea what to do next. He'd tried in every way he knew to show her he loved her. That he was willing to accept her and the children as his own.

He halted, closed his eyes briefly, and sighed. Maybe, just maybe, it wasn't up to him. Maybe he needed to wait, give her time to be ready. Maybe she had to see it for herself.

Trouble was, he wasn't good at waiting. And they'd already waited far too long, in his opinion.

Some of his irritation was ebbing away by the time he reached the grove of trees by the curve in the river. From here he could see the slope of the vines to the south and up to the poplars and firs hugging the shore by his dock. No one was more surprised than he was that he'd become attached to this place. He'd always considered the coast, the hills looking over the Pacific his home. But there was something here he could not deny. And he knew Anna was a large part of it. The guesthouse was done and it was beautiful, he was sure. Everything she did had that sense of flair about it, without being ostentatious. Somehow in the few weeks she'd been here, little things had cropped up...the baskets of flowers hanging from the verandah, a picture on his wall. A pair of shoes left by the door, a toy on the sofa. What Two Willows had been missing was a family. And if they left, it would be all wrong again.

It was his own fault that he'd let his guard down and let her in. And not just her. The wide-eyed wonder of Matteo and the impishness of Aurelia and her cap of soft curls. He didn't want any of them to go. Why couldn't she see this was a second chance for them? He didn't care that the children weren't his. It didn't stop him from loving them. And there was still time for him and Anna to have their own. His heart stopped briefly. What if she were already pregnant? Everything within him seemed to swell, imagining her soft body rounded with the growth of their baby inside her.

He couldn't be done fighting for her yet. There had to be some way to convince her, and he'd find it.

He ran a hand through his hair, and a movement by the dock caught his eye.

Matteo.

The boy was walking carefully along the dock, and Jace watched him with a smile. So precocious, so curious, so completely boy. With all the commotion of the past few days, Jace hadn't been able to take him out in the boat one last time as he'd promised. Matteo made his way to the end of the dock where the boat was tied, and sat, throwing stones from his hand one by one into the water and watching the ripples. He was such a good child. Yes, they'd matched wits in the beginning, but Jace couldn't fault him for wanting to protect his mother, or for seeking attention considering all that had happened. He was smart and he was curious and Jace enjoyed being with him.

Jace started forward...maybe now they could take a short trip up the river. It wasn't much, but Jace did like to think his promises meant something. He'd do this for the boy, and then he'd go back up to the house and try again.

As he started forward, Matteo moved down the dock. Jace hurried his steps. Being on the dock alone wasn't safe. And when Matteo walked over to the side, where the rope for the boat was anchored, Jace's pulse quickened. He should have seen to the ride before now. He should have made good on his promise and taken the time.

"Matteo! Wait!" He called out just as Matteo reached for the rope. Matteo's dark head lifted mid-reach, and he missed the rope. For the briefest moment Jace saw the panic in his eyes as there was nothing for him to grab. Then he toppled into the water.

Jace let out a shout and broke into a run, but already Matteo's head was under the water. His heart pounded— adrenaline and fear. Tiny arms splashed but Matteo was only four. He couldn't swim yet, and Jace knew very well that the end of the dock was well over the boy's head. His legs drove him forward like pistons as he raced towards the dock and dove in, shoes and all.

"Matteo?"

Anna's heart tripped when she realized Matteo wasn't upstairs getting his pajamas on like he'd been told. Aurelia was already asleep, clearly exhausted after frolicking in the river and then sated with a full belly of milk and cookies. But Matteo wasn't in his room. Or in the bathroom. Or downstairs in the kitchen.

Anna checked the backyard and then dashed over to the guesthouse as her unease grew. No Matteo. Her throat closed against the panic rising there. How could this have happened?

She heard voices in her head, ones from the past. Jace, her father, and even Stefano. Especially Stefano, who had mocked her when she'd told him she was divorcing him and taking the children. He'd told her she was a horrible mother. Chills went down her body. He was right. Oh my God, she couldn't find Matteo. She should have known by his attitude that he needed close watching, and instead she'd been only thinking of herself. She jogged back to the house, calling his name.

Then it hit her, and her blood ran cold.

The boat. He'd talked several times today about going in the boat before they left.

"Matteo! Answer Mama!"

She fought back the panic that struggled to overwhelm her, and turned towards the river and the dock. Her boy. Nothing could happen to him. It was impossible. First their baby, and then Stefano...not Matteo too. Anna struggled to take longer breaths. She would find him. He would be fine.

And then she saw them.

Jace coming over the knoll and Matteo in his arms. Anna's heart clubbed painfully. The dark head was against Jace's chest, the tiny arms around his neck, and Jace was dripping, his white shirt nearly transparent and clinging to the hard planes of his body. His lips were set in a grim line, and for one fleeting instant Anna was sure her heart had been ripped clear out of her chest.

And then she heard the muffled sobs, and her relief was so great it nearly dropped her to her knees. Tears rolled down her cheeks as the pieces of the puzzle came together.

The water had taken much from her, and could have again, but for Jace. He was the one she kept coming back to and she knew why. She loved him. She could count on him, always. He was not Stefano. He wasn't weak, in body or spirit. He was

Jace. Her rock. The piece that was missing. And he had saved her son. Not his son. Her son.

She ran forward to meet them, her breath hitching at the sight of the two of them. Jace stopped long enough for her to put her hands on Matteo's cheeks—they were cold—and kiss him.

"He's chilled, but fine. Let's get him inside and dried off."

She nodded dumbly, leaping forward and opening the front door. Jace paused long enough to step out of his ruined shoes and then padded upstairs to Matteo's bedroom.

Matteo was crying quietly, and when Jace put him down he did so gently, kneeling before him. Anna got a towel and Jace wrapped it around Matteo, then pulled him close again into a hug.

"Your mama will look after you."

There was an audible sniff, and Anna saw the arms tighten on Jace's neck. It was too late. Her little boy had already come to love Jace as much as she did.

"*Ti amo*, Jace." The little voice was muffled against the side of Jace's neck but they both heard the words in the language he used when he was afraid. Tears stung her eyes. At times it had been a hard-fought battle between them. But how could she blame Matteo, when she herself loved Jace so completely, despite their mistakes?

"And I love you, Matteo. I'll come back, okay? I need to change my clothes too. I didn't expect to be swimming."

"I'm sorry." Matteo leaned back and looked Jace square in the face. Anna let it unfold. Somehow she knew she had to. They had their own peace to make.

"It wasn't your fault. It was mine. And we'll talk about it later. Right now we both just need to get dry."

"You don't hate me? I am always in the way."

Anna knew Jace had to be grossly uncomfortable in his wet, clinging clothes, but he put it all aside to talk to her son. He took the childish plea seriously. He would be a good father. Perhaps he was right. Perhaps they had all changed. He was already far more tolerant than Stefano had ever been.

Jace leaned over and kissed Matteo's damp head. "I could never hate you, son. You could never do anything that would make me hate you. Remember that."

He stood and met Anna's eyes as the word son vibrated between them. In that moment Anna knew he meant every word. Nothing he could have said would have validated him more in her eyes. He could say all he wanted to her, but she knew he would not lie to her children. He would have expectations but be fair. He would be firm but loving. And now her bags were packed and in the car waiting.

"I need to change," he said quietly and left the room.

Anna turned her attention to Matteo. "Oh, darling. Look at you. Mama was so worried."

"*Mi dispiace*, Mama." His voice was small in the quiet of the bedroom. "I only wanted to say goodbye to the water. I thought I would pull on the rope and see the boat. But I..." tears welled again, "...I fell in."

He flung his arms around her neck. "I was so scared, Mama. I couldn't swim."

Her heart nearly froze, thinking what might have happened if Jace hadn't been there. She squeezed Matteo and then held him back, looking into his white face. "We will have a talk about wandering off and water later." For a moment he looked relieved, so she added, "And we will decide what your punishment should be, Matteo. For now you need to get into your pajamas, nice and dry."

"Yes, Mama."

There was no doubt now in Anna's mind that Jace had saved Matteo's life. The way he'd come striding over the hill like an angel would stay in her memory forever. She hung Matteo's wet clothes over the shower rod in the bathroom to dry, and found him sitting on the bed with Jace when she returned.

Jace looked up at her. "I was just going to tuck him in." He knew it was likely his last chance, unless he could say the right things tonight. He prayed he could. The moment Matteo had toppled into the water, time had stopped. Something new crystallized in Jace's heart. He knew now it was the knowledge that this was his family. He'd called Matteo son and he'd meant it. He'd spent years not wanting a family. Not wanting to hurt like that again, the way he had when he'd come back and Anna had already belonged to someone else. Now he had a chance. He wouldn't give up on these children and he wouldn't give up on her.

He pulled the covers to Matteo's shoulders. "I'll see you in the morning."

Matteo nodded, but Jace saw the tiny quiver in the bottom lip. He leaned forward. "Don't worry," he whispered and winked at the boy. The way Matteo looked up at him nearly broke his heart, a mixture of admiration and love and fear. Someone had to make things right.

Anna kissed her son. "I'm just going to talk to Jace, okay?"

He nodded, but his lashes were already starting to drift down to his cheeks.

Jace let Anna exit the room first, and they walked silently down the steps and out onto the deck, letting the outdoors surround them in a cocoon of privacy.

Jace rested his elbows beside Anna's against the railing,

searching for the words. After several moments they turned to each other, and he had no idea how to say what needed to be said. How to make things right, how to explain what was in his heart.

"I love you."

That was what came out, and it surprised him as much as her. Of all the ways of starting things off, he wasn't expecting that, but it was what came out and Anna's lips dropped open.

"What did you say?"

He rubbed a hand over his face. "I said I love you. I love you and it's the best and worst thing that's ever happened to me. I've loved you since I was sixteen years old and I don't think I could stop if my life depended on it."

She put her fingers to her lips and Jace was sure he'd blown it. He should have said something about Matteo. He should have apologized. He should have—

And then her arms were around him, and he pulled her close and held on.

"Don't leave," he whispered in her ear. "Please don't leave, Anna. I know I'm to blame about Matteo. Stay and I promise I'll spend every day making it up."

She slowly slid her arms back over his shoulders and tilted her head to look up at him.

"What do you mean, you're to blame?"

Meeting her eyes at this moment was one of the hardest things he'd ever done. He'd failed her, and yet he knew he had to tell her, even if it meant losing her. There couldn't be any secrets between them ever again.

"I saw him on the dock. And when he reached for the rope, I called out to him. I thought to make him stop, but when he looked up he lost his balance and..."

He had to swallow hard, couldn't finish the sentence.

"It's my fault. If I'd been here like I promised, we could have gone out on the boat instead of making him wait. I should have put him first. And when I didn't, he nearly..."

He stopped. The alternative was too scary. And still she watched him and waited, her dark eyes piercing into him, a tiny furrow between her eyebrows.

"It isn't your fault, Jace. It was an accident."

He closed his eyes, willing the rest to come out the way he wanted.

"But it never should have happened. When I pulled him out of the water, I could only think of how much you'd already lost. I knew then that you and Matteo and Aurelia mean everything to me. The rest is just...window dressing. And I knew exactly what you meant when you said I wasn't good enough."

His throat tightened painfully as the emotion threatened to take over. He swallowed, blinked. "I failed you in every possible way. But I love you and what I'm asking is for you to give me the chance to make that up."

Anna searched his eyes, knowing he meant every single word he'd uttered. She had no doubt that Matteo's incident had been an accident. But what she was hearing was more wonderful than she ever could have imagined. He loved her. He loved all of them.

When she had been a young girl, Jace had been her hero. He'd been handsome and driven and forbidden. He'd been a safe place and the one she'd trusted to love for the first—and as it turned out—the only time. She had become a woman with him, with a woman's love and a woman's hurt. And now he could be hers again. It was a dizzying, joyous thought.

"You really mean that? You love me."

"Of course I do. How can you doubt it?"

"But you never said it to me before."

He smiled a little, his lips tipping up just a bit, and it made her want to kiss them. But what he was going to say was more important. And she needed the words. Needed to hear them once and for all.

"When we were young, I was afraid. I told myself I wouldn't say it until I was sure I could provide for you. But then when you told me about the baby... I got you the locket and promised myself I would tell you when I gave it to you. But that never happened. You were engaged to Stefano and off-limits. But I never really stopped. I tried. I went out and dated and kept looking for someone who would perhaps take your place. I started this ridiculous competition with your father thinking it would help get you out of my system. But nothing could. I should have known better."

"Why?"

He stepped forward and took her hands. "Because you can't be replaced, Anna. I knew it the night you told me about the baby and we made love again. There will never be anyone for me but you. And now I find myself hoping, just a bit, that you love me again. Because I don't think I can take losing you once more. Not when I love you...and the children...quite so much."

Anna didn't know whether to weep or laugh. "You always said it was about providing for me. And you never understood that I didn't care about those things."

"I was proud. I know it. But growing up, how could I not notice the differences in our households? You with your fancy clothes and servants. And my father a simple laborer. I wanted to deserve you. I wanted to show you I could do it."

"And you did," she said softly.

"Yes, and I'm proud of that. I'm proud of Two Willows. I'm proud that my mother and father are comfortable now and looked after. But I want a family of my own. It all means nothing without you with me, Anna. I want you. And Matteo and Aurelia. They are such beautiful children."

"Are you sure you are ready to be a father, Jace? It's only been a few weeks."

As much as his profession of love meant, she knew she had to put her children first. And so she held her breath, waiting, hoping. She loved him, always had. Now she had to be sure he was ready to commit to her children as well. They needed a father, a real one. She wasn't an innocent girl anymore...she was a package deal. And she wanted it to be true. Wanted to believe.

"If I had any doubts, they vanished when I saw Matteo fall in the river. I have never been that frightened my whole life. I love him as my own. And Aurelia too." He reached for her and cupped her cheek in his hand. "Both of them, and any brothers or sisters that might come along. If you want."

Her heart tripped and started again. "More? You would want more children?"

"I know you might not want to risk it again, after what happened to us before...and I love the children. But if you wanted more..." He paused. "Do you?"

"Well, yes, but—"

"When I came over the knoll with Matteo in my arms, and you were waiting...I felt like I could do anything. This is where we belong. Please, please say you believe it too." He dropped a kiss on her forehead, his breath warm and moist against her skin. "What if you're already pregnant, Anna?"

The thought stopped them both. Anna pressed a hand to

her stomach, wondering. Remembering. And then, with the faintest of glimmers, hoping. Yes, she'd like Jace's child. They deserved that, both of them.

"I am almost afraid to hope," she whispered.

"Just say you love me, Anna, and we'll figure out the rest. I promise."

"I love you."

"Now say you'll marry me."

"I'll marry you."

She pulled back from his arms and looked up, a smile dawning on her face. His expression mirrored hers, wide with wonder and happiness.

"I'll marry you," she repeated, stronger, surer.

As he swung her up in his arms, she knew it didn't matter if she didn't have all the answers. The time had come to trust...in herself, in him. The rest would work itself out.

Epilogue

"Aurelia, could you get me the blanket, please?"

Aurelia picked up the soft pink blanket from the diaper bag and took it to her mother, her long dark curls kissing the tips of her shoulders. She looked very much like Anna had at that age, a fact her Uncle Alex pointed out every time Anna mentioned her daughter's latest precociousness. Anna was now cuddling one-year-old Eva in a rocking chair. "Thank you, Aurelia. You are Mama's good helper."

"Don't forget me!"

Matteo burst through the door, followed by Jace.

"Yes, of course." These days Matteo's help was less with the baby and more around the vineyards, but Anna loved seeing him follow in Jace's footsteps.

"Papa says we can get the boat ready tomorrow." He went to Anna's chair and put a finger on Eva's cheek. "You wait, Eva. Papa says I can drive."

He was rewarded with a sleepy grin.

"Room for three more?"

Four heads turned towards the door.

"Uncle Alex!" Matteo's cry rang out and he ran to his uncle. "You can come on the boat with us tomorrow."

Alex laughed and drew Melissa inside with him. Their

daughter, Laura, peeked out from mahogany-colored bangs, a thumb popped in her mouth.

"Matteo is more than happy for male company. I think he feels overrun with girls." Jace came forward, hugged Alex and ruffled Matteo's hair.

"Let me take her," Alex said, lifting Laura from Melissa's arms.

Melissa sighed, rested her hand on her significantly rounded stomach, and lifted her cheek for a kiss from her brother-in-law. "I'm so glad we could come for the weekend. Alex says I'm not allowed to travel after next week."

Anna shared a look that clearly said, "Men," even though she knew they both secretly adored being doted upon.

"And your father?" Jace put the question to Alex, who answered with a sober shake of his head.

"I'm afraid not."

Roberto Morelli had refused to attend Jace and Anna's wedding, and his relationship with Alex was tenuous at best.

"Our father is too proud for his own good," Anna replied.

But Jace saw beneath her pronouncement to the hurt. "I'm sorry, Anna."

Anna looked into Jace's eyes. After all the years of resentment, he'd swallowed his pride and gone to Morelli to speak to her father, to ask for his blessing and to put the past behind them. She loved him for trying, even if her father had refused to even open the door. "It's not your fault, Jace," she said softly.

Alex broke the dismal mood by clapping his hands together. "Okay, okay, enough of this—cookies and milk with Uncle Alex in the kitchen. You too." He aimed a glance at Melissa. "You need your milk."

Aurelia and Matteo disappeared with the Morellis at the promise of sweets, and Jace leaned over to give Anna a kiss.

"You're sure you're up to this?"

Anna laughed. "Are you sure you are? You've got a full house for a few days."

"There's always room for family."

Anna thought back to barely two years previous, when Jace had been a bachelor and things hadn't been nearly so rosy. "There really is, isn't there?"

"But...I don't want you to wear yourself out."

She grinned. "I'm fine. And Alex will help for a few days."

"Yes, but that was before—"

"Before three children and a son on the way?"

She patted her rounded belly and her smile widened at Jace's expression.

"A son? You know?"

"I found out last week. But I wanted it to be a surprise."

"A son..."

"And a brother for Matteo." It had been a bone of contention for a few months when Eva had turned out to be a sister and not the brother Matteo had requested. "I don't want you to overdo it, Anna. We can hire help."

Anna nodded. It no longer bothered her to think of the children having a nanny. Jace was not Stefano. But she worked from home now, running the wine shop and taking care of the accommodations for the guesthouse. She enjoyed seeing the happy faces of her children during her day and taking them for walks in the afternoons. The children came first. And when Jace came in from among the vines...

"If I need help, I'll be sure to ask. The only help I need right now is putting the children to bed. And after that..."

"And after that, *Signora* Willow?"

The promise was clear in his voice and she closed her eyes for a moment. She was so lucky. So blessed to have him as her husband and her best friend. In so many ways, her life had been waiting for her. Like a bottle of Two Willows Syrah, all the flavors and notes and tones locked inside until Jace had uncorked it. With Jace she had the freedom to breathe, and with that freedom came unexpected richness, full and satisfying.

She tipped her head up for a kiss, tasted him on her lips and smiled.

"And after that..." he murmured, questioning.

The moment held, perfect.

"After that," she whispered softly, "is forever."

About the Author

A busy wife and mother of three (2 daughters and the family dog), Donna Alward believes hers is the best job in the world; a combination of stay-at-home mom and romance novelist.

An avid reader since childhood, Donna always made up her own stories. She completed her Arts Degree in English Literature in 1994, but it wasn't until 2001 that she penned her first full-length novel, and found herself hooked on writing romance. In 2006 she sold her first manuscript, and is now an award-winning author of more than a dozen romances.

From her home office in Nova Scotia, Canada, Donna loves being back on the East Coast after nearly 12 years in Alberta where her career began.

To learn more about Donna Alward, please visit www.donnaalward.com, check out her blog at www.donnaalward.blogspot.com, or join her newsletter. Send an email to Donna at donnaalward@hotmail.com.

All she wants is his name on the dotted line.
He's got other ideas...

Sold to the Highest Bidder
© *2010 Donna Alward*

For Ella, marrying Devin had seemed like a good idea at the time. Friends since childhood and in love with him for as long as she could remember, marriage had been the next logical step. Then the real world called, and Ella's feet had itched to get out of Backwards Gulch, Colorado.

Now, with a new opportunity on the East Coast beckoning, it's time to put her past behind her once and for all. When she sees Devin standing on a charity auction block, she decides it's the perfect opportunity to finally get his signature on the divorce papers he never signed.

Devin's certain about one thing when he sees Ella for the first time in twelve years—she's not the girl he married. The way she left him still stings, and if she wants him to sign on the dotted line he's going to make her work for it...for the full forty-eight hours she paid for.

When the old attraction flares between them, the years apart disappear and resolve melts faster than high-country snow in summer. But when Ella awakens with the same determination to get back to Denver, divorce papers in hand, she has a problem...

Devin still hasn't signed them.

Warning: Bourbon shooters, shirtless cowboys, and a hot rendezvous or two...

Available now in ebook and print from Samhain Publishing.

Enjoy the following excerpt from Sold to the Highest Bidder...

Ella scrambled to write her check and hurry outside, her heels clicking furiously on the scratched wood floor. The article had slipped to a corner of her mind. She knew Ruby Shoes and its patrons well enough to fudge that part of the article. She ignored the calls from old neighbors and long-ago acquaintances. What she really wanted to know was where Dev had gone. And how on earth she could convince him to sign the papers so she could leave this backwoods town behind her forever. He *owed* her now. She had just made sure of it by buying him off the stage. He was at her beck and call for forty-eight hours. All she wanted would take a few seconds.

The air outside had cooled and it kissed her skin, damp from the close atmosphere inside the bar. Her feet halted abruptly. Dev was leaning against the tailgate of his pickup truck, the same two-tone brown Lariat he'd driven to the courthouse on their wedding day. It had several more dents and rust spots now. He'd put his shirt back on. Thank God. Because seeing all those planes and angles while he'd flashed that knowing dimple at her had been torture. It had brought back memories she'd rather stayed buried.

She didn't want to be married to him any more. That had nothing to do with the fact that seeing him strip off his shirt had made her want to touch him. Taste him. Make love to him. It was plumb crazy, but her libido had spoken loud and clear—it was listening to her memory, not her head.

A small grin curled up the side of his mouth and her breasts tightened. She needed him to sign the decree. Now. So she'd never have to see him and his sexy grin again. So she could finally move on.

"What are you doing here, Ella?"

His voice was a little soft, a little rough, and it rode the endings of her nerves, sending shivers up her spine. She straightened her shoulders. There was no way on God's green earth she would let him know he got to her in any way. And he sure didn't want to spend two days with her. Not once in twelve years had he made any effort to see her whatsoever. She'd let him off the hook all for the price of his name beside the X.

She lifted her chin, tucked her notebook more firmly into her handbag. "Does it matter?"

He nodded, slowly. "You bet your designer bag it does. And I'm pretty sure paying two thousand dollars for two days with me wasn't the reason. Though we could have a lot of fun in two days, don't you think? For old times' sake?"

Memories of bygone days swirled around her, seducing. "Shut up, Dev," she murmured.

He boosted himself away from the truck and came closer. She could smell his woodsy aftershave, feel his body invade her personal space and hated herself for liking it. Craving it.

He leaned into her ear while the hairs on her neck stood up from the close contact of his breath on her skin.

"You could have had me for free."

She planted her hands on his shoulders and pushed, skittering away on her heels. "I...I was sent on a story. It had nothing to do with you, you egomaniac."

He snorted, looking at the ground and scuffing it with the toe of a sorry looking boot. "A story. Of course. Makes sense to send a big-city reporter to a dive like Ruby's for some trumped-up charity event."

He wouldn't understand. He never had. This was why she'd sent him divorce papers several times, even back when the legal fees to do so meant she had to eat peanut butter for a few weeks. "There's something bigger at work than Betty Tucker's illness, you know." She straightened her blouse and raised an eyebrow at him. Damn straight. There was corruption from the top down, and Betty Tucker was only one victim. Bringing an exposé against Betty's insurance company would guarantee Ella her choice of assignment.

"I bet Betty Tucker wouldn't think so. Do you think a woman who might be dying cares at all about how many newspapers get sold in Denver?"

Damn him. He'd always had a way of making her feel small when that wasn't what she'd meant at all. Couldn't he see it was a greater-good issue? But Dev had never been one to see the big picture. He'd had the most annoying tunnel vision of anyone she ever met. Right and wrong. Black and white.

"I don't expect you to understand," she huffed, lifting her nose and moving to walk past him to her car. Forty-eight hours. Hmph. If he'd sign by the X right now, he'd be off the hook and she'd consider it two thousand dollars well spent. They could end this farce of a marriage and get on to their respective lives.

He reached out and grabbed her arm.

"You never expected me to understand, Ell." The words were laced with unexpected venom. "I understand a hell of a lot more than you think."

His fingers burned holes in her sleeve and she fought back the thrill of excitement thrumming through her just by having his hands on her again. It shouldn't happen after all this time, but he'd always had that effect on her. She pasted on the brightest smile she could muster. "Brilliant. So why don't you tell me what I'm thinking right now?"

He still had a firm grip on her biceps and she tilted her chin way up to look at him. Even with her heels on, he was taller than her. Over six feet of manly sexiness. Her gaze caught on his lips. Those lips had known every inch of her when they'd been little more than kids. She blinked. Back then he'd been the solution, not the problem. The savior, not the devil.

"You're thinking, how am I going to get Dev to sign those papers I've got sitting in my car?"

She twisted out of his grip and stomped to the car as his knowing laughter echoed behind her. She *had* been thinking exactly that. Along with wondering how his mouth would feel over hers when she wanted nothing more than to be free of him. For good. How was it possible to think both at the same time?

"Well. You're smarter than you look," she answered, determined he not know the effect he was having on her. If ever she'd needed confirmation that she'd done the right thing by not looking back, here it was staring her in the face. She couldn't even manage a simple conversation with him without losing perspective.

"Yep. So where to now, Ell? Because according to your terms of purchase, we've got forty-eight whole hours."

A shiver went through her at the possibilities. But possibilities got a girl absolutely nowhere. "You sign these now, and we'll call it even. Both of us free as a bird."

He came towards her, walking with that lazy long stride she remembered. His T-shirt was untucked and had a line of dust across it from the floor inside. She wanted to reach up and brush it off. But she didn't. She couldn't touch him. Not after the way her body had reacted when he'd whispered in her ear.

She backed up against the door of her car, her breath hardly moving her chest.

"I'm in no rush, Ella McQuade."

"You never were." She said it with a snarky twist so he'd be sure to get the insult. "And don't call me that."

His body was warm as they hovered only inches apart. If she leaned forward the slightest bit they'd be touching in several places. Her body strained against her clothing while her head warned her to stay put.

"Why not? It's your name."

"Not anymore."

He lifted his hand and traced a finger down her sleeve. She shivered. He'd always been that way. He'd always known what a simple touch could do to her. They'd learned together, discovering all the special spots. Only now it was worse. Now they were older, wiser. Knowing he still had that effect on her hurt. She should have moved on by now. Moving on was the entire reason she'd brought those papers to begin with.

"It is until I sign those."

"Please, just sign them then. Sign them and I'll be out of your hair for good."

His finger went up her sleeve and down again. "Not yet. Come back to the house. I still have some things of yours anyway. You can pick them up."

"Devin." She looked up at him, censoring him with her eyes. "You know that's not a good idea."

Dammit, saying it did nothing more than give credence to the attraction shimmering between them.

"When have you and I ever had good ideas?"

The door to Ruby's opened and shut again and she sighed. Did she really want to argue this in a public place?

"Almost never," she admitted.

"Forty-eight hours. That's my deal, Ell. You spend the weekend with me, and at the end of it I'll sign your precious papers. You'll be free as a bird, as you said."

CPSIA information can be obtained at www.ICGtesting.com
263871BV00002B/1/P